THE STARTUP SQUAD

PARTY PROBLEMS

By Brian Weisfeld and Nicole C. Kear

【Imprint】
MAKE YOUR MARK

New York

[Imprint]
MAKE YOUR MARK

A part of Macmillan Publishing Group, LLC
120 Broadway, New York, NY 10271

Library of Congress Cataloging-in-Publication Data is available.

ISBN 978-1-250-83867-4 (paperback) / ISBN 978-1-250-18050-6 (ebook)

Our books may be purchased in bulk for promotional, educational, or business use. Please contact your local bookseller or the Macmillan Corporate and Premium Sales Department at (800) 221-7945 ext. 5442 or by email at MacmillanSpecialMarkets@macmillan.com.

Book design by Elynn Cohen

Imprint logo designed by Amanda Spielman

First edition, 2021

1 3 5 7 9 10 8 6 4 2

mackids.com

"Don't move!" Didi called to Harriet.

She'd been adjusting Harriet's position for five minutes, and now, at long last, it was perfect. Harriet leaned against the big oak tree in Didi's backyard, her knees drawn up and her hands behind her head. Didi was ready to sketch her.

Harriet was a fantastic model—her big, bold expressions made her fun to draw, and her body language was always interesting. But she seemed incapable of sitting still even for a minute.

Case in point: As soon as Didi put pencil to paper,

Harriet jumped up and ran over to peer over Didi's shoulder.

"I just want to see how it's going." Harriet frowned. "No offense, Di, but it doesn't look like me at *all*."

"Yeah, because I haven't even started," Didi said. The page was blank except for an oval for Harriet's face, a neck, and the beginnings of shoulders. "Can you try to sit exactly the way I had you?"

"Sure thing, boss." Harriet saluted her, and Didi had to laugh. Harriet could be exasperating, but she was impossible to stay mad at.

No sooner had Harriet assumed her tree-leaning, head-tilted, Mona Lisa–smile posture, she let out a howl.

"Ahhhhhh!" Harriet screamed as a tennis ball bounced off her forehead. She grabbed her head and threw herself onto the grass, rolling back and forth.

"I'm bleeding!" she yelled. "Am I bleeding?"

Resa and Amelia jogged over from where they'd been practicing volleys in Didi's driveway. Amelia grabbed the tennis ball and leaned over to examine Harriet's head.

"Sorry, Harriet," she said. "But I think you're okay."

"The good news is that your backhand is killer, Amelia," said Resa, smiling. "The bad news is, I mean that literally."

"It's a work in progress," said Amelia. "Like your teaching skills."

"I need ice," Harriet moaned. "To control the swelling."

"I'll get some," Amelia offered.

"And some more iced tea," Harriet went on. "I'm parched."

"Coming up," said Didi, closing her sketchbook. The portrait session was obviously over. Maybe she'd try again next Sunday.

Didi grabbed the empty pitcher from the table on the patio and opened the screen door that led into the kitchen. Amelia followed behind her.

"Didn't get too far with the portrait, huh?" asked Amelia.

"I mostly just needed to get a rough human figure for this design I'm working on," said Didi. "But yeah, I didn't even make it to the elbows."

"Elbows are overrated," said Amelia.

"If I could download PictureHouse, it wouldn't be a problem," said Didi. "I'd just upload a picture of Harriet, and then I could trace what I needed in, like, two seconds."

Didi pulled an ice-cube tray from the freezer and overturned it onto a plate, releasing an abundance of ice cubes.

"That sounds like a cool app," Amelia said. "You should get it."

Didi dropped the ice cubes into the pitcher.

"I would," Didi said, "but the subscription is super expensive."

She pulled out a large plastic container full of tea from the fridge and poured it over the ice.

The screen door creaked, and Harriet staggered in, collapsing in a kitchen chair.

"How bad is the bump?" she asked the girls. "Be honest. Scale of one to ten."

"I told her it was a zero," Resa said, trailing behind her. "She doesn't believe me."

"Here." Amelia handed Harriet a Ziploc bag full of ice. "This should help."

"This, too." Didi placed a fresh glass of iced tea, with extra honey to satisfy Harriet's sweet tooth, in front of her. Then she filled a glass bowl with cheese crackers and placed it in the middle of the table. Didi's mother believed in good manners, and she'd taught Didi that when guests came over, you always offered food, even if it was only cheese crackers.

"Hey, Didi," said Amelia, filling her own glass with tea. "Maybe PictureHouse has a student discount. You should check."

"They do," said Didi. "Even with that, it costs $114 a year."

Amelia whistled. "Steep."

"It's less than the price of a guitar," said Resa, taking a long drink of the icy-cold tea.

"That is a true but random fact," said Amelia.

"Not random," corrected Resa. "When we sold Skinks merch, we made enough in one week to pay for a new electric guitar *and* drums for the band."

"Yeah, and the boys *still* won't let me come into their room!" Harriet pouted. "Which makes me seriously regret handing over all that money to them! I should've given it to my mom to pay for a new salon chair."

Didi handed the girls coasters to put under their glasses.

"What's wrong with your mom's salon chair?" Didi asked, sitting down next to Harriet.

"What isn't wrong with it?" Harriet asked. "The seat part hasn't gone up or down for years, and then the boys were playing hockey in the basement and broke off one of the armrests. Plus, Zappa—"

Didi shuddered. Even the mention of that reptile's name brought back the feeling of Zappa's cold body on her head. A few weeks before, when Didi was at Harriet's house, the pet skink had made a great escape and taken a wrong turn into Didi's long brown hair.

"What'd Zappa do this time?" Amelia laughed.

"She's pulled out the stuffing inside the seat!" Harriet exclaimed. "There's hardly any left! It's her favorite game now."

"You *could* keep her in a cage," suggested Resa with raised eyebrows.

"Would you keep Stella in a cage?" Harriet replied. Stella was Resa's schnauzer—a sweet and devoted dog that Harriet, a natural animal lover, was very fond of.

"No, but Stella doesn't eat salon chairs and get tangled in people's hair," Resa pointed out.

"Well, it's too late now anyway," said Harriet. "The chair's a goner. And she needs a new one so she can see clients in the basement. And they're expensive!"

"I could use some cash, too," said Amelia, tossing a cheese cracker into her mouth. "I'm visiting my dad, back in the city, next month."

Didi was intrigued. Amelia didn't talk about her dad much. All Didi knew was that Amelia had moved to town a few months earlier when her mom got a job as the editor of the local paper and that her dad had stayed behind. He'd visited a few times, for the weekend, but Didi hadn't met him yet.

"I'm going clothes shopping with my old friends—and there's a concert we want to see and a makeup store that just opened." Amelia sighed. "I need spending money, and I'm broke."

"Me too," said Resa. "Which is really bad timing because Bounce Back! is having its annual fundraiser.

I always donate—every year. I can't break the tradition now."

"Bounce Back!?" asked Amelia.

"It's a charity," Resa explained. "They give tennis rackets to kids who can't afford one. I'm the president of the local chapter."

"That's such a cool idea," said Amelia. "If I had any money, I'd donate."

"Look at us," Harriet said glumly. She shoved a handful of crackers into her mouth and chomped. "Just four broke girls. We make money for *everyone* else—our school, the Skinks—but when *we* need money, who helps us?"

Resa paused, on the verge of popping a cracker into her mouth.

"We do," she said.

"We do what?" Harriet asked.

"We help ourselves." Resa turned to the other girls, getting excited. "If we need money, we'll just start up the Startup Squad again."

"And do what?" Didi pushed her tortoiseshell eyeglasses up to the bridge of her nose. "Another concert?"

Resa shook her head. "Those Skinks fans are waaaaay too much drama. And so are the Skinks."

"I know *exactly* what we should sell!" Harriet nearly jumped out of her chair. "I have the perfect idea for a skink toy."

"I just said we shouldn't do band merch," said Resa.

"Not Skinks the band," said Harriet, smiling. "Skinks the skinks."

"Are you understanding this?" Resa asked Amelia.

"Remember how I said Zappa loves pulling the stuffing out of my mom's salon chair?" Harriet asked. "Well, I figured she was bored, so I tried to get her to stop by buying her a skink chew toy. I thought she'd like something hard on the outside but soft on the inside, like the salon chair. And there's nothing! It doesn't exist! If we made one, we'd make a fortune!"

"A skink chew toy?" asked Resa, who was struggling to hide her skepticism. "How many people even own skinks?"

"Four million," said Harriet. "Give or take."

Amelia was typing on her phone and scrolling through the results of her web search.

"Um, not quite," she said. "I found the National Skinks Owner Society, and it has . . ." She looked up. "Twenty members."

"You know what there *are* a lot of, though?" Resa chimed in. "People who want to learn tennis. Especially in this town."

"That's true," said Amelia. "In the city, I barely even played table tennis. But here, it's the thing to do."

"And private tennis lessons cost a fortune," Resa went on. "It's a total rip-off! Seventy-five dollars an hour? For someone whose serve is mediocre at best?"

"They're expensive, all right," Amelia agreed.

"I could charge a lot less and teach people a lot more!" Resa concluded. "People would line up around the block to hire me. We'd be rolling in money."

"Uhhh," said Amelia.

"What?" asked Resa, crossing her arms in front of her. "You don't think I'm good at tennis?"

"Oh, I think you're good at *tennis*," said Amelia. "I just don't know how good you are at *teaching*."

Didi's shoulders tensed. She hated it when people argued, especially two of her good friends. Resa and Amelia had been getting along a lot better lately: In fact, they seemed to have become close. Still, they both could be stubborn and occasionally clashed. Didi was always on high alert for these moments.

"I am a *great* teacher!" Resa protested. "I push hard, and the payoff is huge!"

"Right," said Amelia. "It's just the *fun* part that's missing."

Didi offered the bowl of cheese crackers to Resa and said, "When I'm with you, the fun part is never missing!"

"Thanks, Di." Resa smiled, then turned to Amelia. "So I guess you have a better idea?"

"I've got something in mind," said Amelia. "It's cooking."

"Cooking?" Resa asked, eyebrows raised.

"Yeah, cooking," said Amelia. "Not ready yet. I don't want to serve you undercooked ideas."

Didi laughed. "Please don't."

"But let me ask you all a question." Amelia tucked her hair behind her ears, even though it was already perfectly in place. "When you're on ImageFest and you see influencers advertising products, is it annoying?"

"Oh, you mean like how Karley Key posted this morning about that gross power drink?" Harriet made a revolted face. "I tried that stuff a while ago, when Sam was drinking it, trying to bulk up for football."

Didi laughed at the thought of Harriet's skinny, not-very-coordinated older brother playing football.

"First of all, it was *the* most disgusting beverage I've ever tasted," said Harriet. "And second of all, it didn't work! If anything, Sam got skinnier and had *less* energy. It was a scam!"

"So you *did* mind when Karley Key posted about it?" Amelia was confused.

Harriet shook her head. "No. That video she made about it was totally hilarious."

"Yeah, and it was obvious that it was an ad," said

Resa. "The part where she was like, 'I feed it to my tigers,' had me rolling."

Harriet cracked up. Her two high pigtails shook like pom-poms as she laughed.

"What I don't like is when celebrities try to act like it's not an ad," said Didi. "Because then it feels like a lie. Like you're being tricked."

"Right," said Amelia, nodding.

"Why?" asked Resa. "You thinking of becoming an influencer?"

"Definitely not," said Amelia.

"Okay, so we've got zero ideas from Amelia, then," said Resa. "A chew toy for the least popular pet in America—"

"Objection, Your Honor!" protested Harriet.

"Sustained!" Didi replied, laughing.

"And my idea," said Resa. "Coaching lessons for tennis players that they can actually afford."

"You forgot Didi," Amelia pointed out, turning to her friend. "What do you have?"

Didi knew she wanted to build a side business around her art someday, after college, but that was as far as she'd taken the idea. Right in this moment, she had no genius plans for a business. She felt, as she often did when the girls convened, that they moved forward with their plans so quickly she hardly had a chance to catch up, much less lead the way. She knew she could figure out a solid business idea, but she needed time to think it through.

"I've got something cooking, too," she said. "It's . . . simmering."

"Well, turn up the heat!" Resa encouraged her. "We need a fully cooked idea!"

Easy for Resa to say. She was fast about everything. She'd already drained her glass of iced tea and eaten most of the cheese crackers in the bowl.

Now she was on her feet, spinning the tennis racket in her hand.

"C'mon, Amelia," she said. "I'm declaring a state of emergency for your backhand. We've got to fix it before it actually knocks someone unconscious."

Amelia got to her feet but raised her eyebrows at Harriet and Didi. "See what I mean?"

"Hey, Didi," said Harriet. "Instead of a portrait against a tree, what about a portrait of me eating that slice of pizza I saw in your fridge?"

"How about we keep the pizza, lose the portrait?" asked Didi with a smile.

Harriet sighed with relief. "I thought you'd never ask."

When Didi got home from yearbook meeting the next afternoon, the house was filled with the mouth-watering smell of sizzling ginger-garlic.

"Indira?" her mother called.

Didi walked into the kitchen and found her mom at the stove, tending three pans at once. Her mother's wavy brown hair was pulled into a neat bun at the base of her neck, and her apron looked spotless despite that she'd obviously been cooking for a long time. Her mother was always tidy and well-ordered, and she kept her home the same way.

"What are you making?" Didi asked.

"Butter chicken and rice," her mother replied. "And your father asked for chole bhature."

"Yum," said Didi. Chole bhature was one of her favorites—a tangy chickpea curry eaten with the fluffiest rounds of fried bread. No one made it quite as scrumptious as her Naani in Delhi did, but her mother did a pretty great job nonetheless.

"Wash your hands, and stir this, please," her mom said. "If it sticks, it will be ruined."

Didi scrubbed her hands at the kitchen sink— warm water, plenty of soap, backs and in between the fingers, too.

"How was school?" Mrs. Singh asked as she lifted a puffy mound of dough out from under a dishcloth where it had been left to rise.

"It was good." Didi inserted a wooden spoon into the bubbling pot. "I helped Mr. Ewoja prep his sculpture project for the first graders. They're making clay birds. It's so cute."

"I remember when you made your bird in first grade," said her mom, as she pinched off small pieces of dough and rolled them into perfect balls between her palms. "A falcon. It was incredible. I remember I showed it to Kavita Auntie, and she called me a liar. She said it was impossible a seven-year-old could create such a thing."

"C'mon, Maa," said Didi. "It wasn't that good."

"Don't argue with your mother," her mom said,

pretending to scold her. "If I say you're a genius, then you are a genius."

"I just wish I could make some money from my art," said Didi.

Her mother looked up, alarmed. "Why do you need money, Indira?"

"I don't *need* money," Didi said. "There's just a software program I want, that's all. And it's kind of pricey. So I thought maybe I could start a little business—"

Her mother had turned her attention back to the bhature dough. She was shaking her head.

"No, Indira," she said. "It is not a good idea. You need to focus on school."

"Yeah, I know," Didi jumped in quickly. "I was just thinking of a really small side business, you know, for the weekends and after school, when I'm done with my homework."

Her mother was pursing her lips and flattening the little balls of dough with a large rolling pin. She glanced up at Didi, and nodded her head at the pot. "Keep stirring."

Didi rotated the spoon around the pot. "You know how Baba is always talking about Sheila Orbacher?"

Her father was in the process of reading his third book by the financial whiz Sheila Orbacher and he was a mega fan. He was always offering up little nuggets of Orbacher wisdom, at breakfast . . . and dinner . . . and plenty of times in between.

"I think he's right," Didi continued. "It's good to build some business sense early on. Plus"—she raised her eyebrows to emphasize her point—"it would look great on my college applications."

If something could be put on a college application, Didi had learned, her mother was far more inclined to approve of it.

"Maybe it would be all right, if it was just a small job." Her mother nodded as she rolled the dough. "Maybe Linda at the shop needs help on the weekends."

"Maybe," Didi said, peering into the bubbling pot. She was thinking that, as an only child, her mother already paid enough attention to her every move. She didn't exactly relish the idea of spending more time with her in the close quarters of Linda's flower shop, where her mom worked.

Then her mother gasped. She dropped the roller so abruptly, it rolled right off the counter onto the floor.

"I have an idea!" she announced.

"Maa," said Didi, gesturing to the pot, "I think this is ready—"

Her mother was beaming.

"It is perfect! I don't know why I didn't think of it before!"

"What's perfect?"

"I will call Kavita Auntie now!"

Her mother turned to leave the kitchen as Didi called, "Maa—wait! What about all these pots?"

"Just keep stirring!" her mother called over her shoulder as she vanished into the living room.

~~~~~~

An hour later, Didi sat in her chair at the dining room table, in between her parents, while her mother spooned out large mounds of steaming jasmine rice, and her father passed around the plate of chole bhature.

"It's all settled!" her mother announced. "You have a job!"

"Wait, what?" Didi tried to mask her annoyance that, once again, her mother had committed her to doing something without asking her first. Her mom always meant well, but she tended to get carried away and sometimes forgot that Didi was not a toddler anymore. "What's the job?"

"You will design an invitation for Haresh Uncle's birthday party!" her mother went on.

Kavita was Mrs. Singh's oldest friend, and Haresh was Kavita's husband. They were like family to Didi, and she knew they'd never refuse any of her mother's requests, which made her feel like it wasn't so much a job as charity.

"Haresh Uncle is turning fifty," Mrs. Singh went on. "And Kavita Auntie is throwing him a surprise party, but she didn't like any of the invitations she saw at the drugstore. She was just complaining to me about this yesterday, so I told her when I called just now that my genius daughter can make her exactly what she wants!"

"Maa, I've never done anything like this," Didi protested.

"You designed a T-shirt," her father pointed out. "And that is even harder."

"Don't worry. Kavita Auntie gave you instructions." She fished a piece of paper out of her pocket and read it. "The invitations must be sophisticated but not boring. Formal but not too formal—the party is at their house. And please include orchids."

"Perfect," grumbled Didi under her breath. It sounded impossible.

"Indira, you're letting your food get cold," her mother chastised. "Eat, eat!"

After dinner, when Didi started loading the dishwasher, her mother shooed her out of the kitchen and told her to get to work on the invitation. It took Didi a few hours, and plenty of sketch paper, but by the next morning, she had three possible designs to run by Kavita, all featuring orchids of various shapes and sizes.

She showed them to her mom at breakfast the next morning, and her mother was delighted.

"These are even better than I thought!" Mrs. Singh passed them to her husband. "If I had known, I would have charged her more. This beautiful invitation for just fifty dollars? A steal!"

Didi froze, her slice of buttered toast halfway to her lips.

"Fifty dollars?" she repeated.

"Yes, I know." Her mother shook her head. "I should have charged more."

"Maa!" Didi exclaimed. "I thought you charged her fifteen dollars, maybe twenty dollars. Fifty dollars is too much!"

"Do you know what Sheila Orbacher says?" her father asked, looking up from the sketches.

Didi wondered for the umpteenth time when her father would tire of the business whiz and move on to a new author, someone who, hopefully, wasn't so quotable.

"If you don't know your own worth," her dad intoned, "no one else will, either."

"That is true." Mrs. Singh nodded. "I will take these to Kavita Auntie on my way to work and see which one—oh!" Didi's mom stopped buttering a slice of toast and turned to her daughter. "I have the most wonderful idea for your next job!"

"Maa, wait—"

"Eat your breakfast!" Mrs. Singh called as she raced upstairs to her bedroom.

"Maa, can you—" Didi turned to her father. "Do you have any idea what she's signing me up for now?"

Her father shook his head. "You never know with your mother. But—" He looked brightly at his daughter. "Sheila Orbacher's first rule of success is to never say *no* to the unknown."

"Easy for Sheila Orbacher to say," muttered Didi.

"Hey, Didi!" Resa greeted her friend as Didi rushed through the door of homeroom. Resa was seated at the table she shared with Didi, Amelia, Harriet, and a few other classmates. "Cutting it a little close today, huh?"

Didi looked up at the clock on the wall. There was still three minutes before homeroom officially started.

"I'm not late."

Resa laughed. "I'm joking, Di. It's just that you're always the first one through the door—after Miss

Punctual over there." She gestured at Val, who stood at Ms. Davis's desk. This was Val's default position in the mornings. She had crowned herself teacher's assistant and was always doing something helpful for Ms. Davis before anyone else arrived. Today, she was writing the week's announcements on the whiteboard. She'd written *TOMORROW: STUDENT GOVERNMENT MEETING 3 pm, AUDITORIUM (with moi!).*

"The way she acts, you'd think she had been president of the country, not of the fifth grade," said Resa disdainfully. "I'd like to run against her for class president this year—show her she doesn't have the election all sewn up like she thinks she does."

Didi tossed her backpack onto the table and plopped down in her seat.

"Well, elections are coming up," she said. "And you know she's probably been planning her campaign for months."

"Yeah." Resa turned to look at her friend. "Why are you late, anyway?"

"I got a late start," Didi said. "My mom decided this morning was the perfect time to jump-start my art career."

"Details, please." Resa's bright eyes shone, and she tapped her toes, clad in red Converse, on the floor in anticipation. Resa loved a good story.

Didi explained how she'd taken on designing an invitation last night and how her mother had been so pleased with the result that she'd already secured another job for her.

"What's the job?" Resa asked.

"Okay, so my cousins—"

"The triplets?" Resa clarified.

"Yeah, the triplets," Didi said. "Well, their mother's best friend, Agnes—you know Agnes, right?"

"Uhhh, I think so," Resa said, furrowing her brow. "The woman who does Shakespeare in random places all over town in the summer?"

"Yeah, with her theater troupe, Bard Without Barriers."

Agnes was an actor. A very serious actor. She'd grown up in town, then studied theater at a fancy conservatory in the city. After she graduated, she decided to move back home and start a Shakespearean site-specific theatrical troupe. In the summer, they put on productions in unexpected places—*Henry V* in the parking lot, *Macbeth* on the golf course.

"Remember that production of *Romeo and Juliet* they did in the playground?" asked Resa, chuckling.

"I don't," said Amelia, who'd just walked through the door and was lowering herself into a chair. "Fill me in."

"It was . . ." Even if Agnes wasn't there to hear her, Didi, who was unfailingly diplomatic, didn't feel comfortable insulting her play. "It was memorable."

"It was a *disaster*," said Resa. "Agnes played Juliet. She climbed to the top of the monkey bars to do the balcony scene, but it had been raining—"

"No!" gasped Amelia. "She slipped?"

"Yeah," said Resa. "They had to stop the play to take her to the hospital and everything. Big-time drama."

"Thankfully, she didn't break anything," Didi hastened to add.

"So, wait—what happened with your mom this morning?" asked Resa. She pulled down the red stretchy headband she wore to keep the curls out of her eyes, then pushed it back into place. "Don't tell me she volunteered you to be in one of Agnes's plays?"

"No!" Didi exclaimed. The thought of performing filled her with horror. "No, it's not that bad. Agnes is getting married—to Rick, actually. He's also in the theater troupe—"

"No *way*!" Resa exclaimed, earning a stern look from Ms. Davis. Their homeroom teacher let them chat and joke around in the morning, but she didn't let things get loud. "Rick was *Romeo*!"

"Ooooh, a backstage romance." Amelia laughed.

"So, anyway," Didi pressed on, "she's getting

married to Rick and needs someone to design the place cards for the wedding, and my mom said I'd do it." She frowned.

"So what's the problem?" asked Resa. "You don't like Agnes?"

"No, Agnes is really nice," Didi said. "It's just . . . I don't know anything about place cards."

"What's to know?" Amelia shrugged. "They're little cards. They have names on them. They tell people what table to sit at at parties."

"Parties!" Harriet plopped down next to Amelia, panting. Harriet always panted in the morning because she was always running, and she was always running because she was always late. "I love parties!"

"Hey, Harriet," Resa said. "You've got a whole minute and a half left in homeroom."

"That much?" Harriet smiled, smoothing out her freshly braided black hair. "I must've run faster than I thought."

"Didi's doing stationery design for a wedding," explained Amelia.

Harriet clapped her hands together. "Weddings! One of my favorite kinds of parties! Can I come?"

Didi laughed. "Oh, nobody's going—I mean, I'm not going, either. I'm just designing the place cards. It's not a big deal."

But it soon became clear that her little design gig was a bigger deal than she thought.

Agnes was not the problem. Agnes was friendly and easy to work with. Didi spoke with her on the phone that evening, after dinner.

"So the theme for the wedding," Agnes said, enunciating her words in a way that struck Didi as very actor-like, "is Shakespeare!"

"Okay, great," said Didi, taking notes in her sketchbook. "Can you give me, maybe, an example?"

"Yes, of course, absolutely," Agnes said. "Our wedding's going to be in the Kings Hotel. The ceremony will take place on the stage in the theater. Then we'll move into the ballroom for the reception. We're going to have red velvet and brocade everywhere! I want it to ooze opulence!"

"Opulence," Didi repeated, scribbling it in her book. "Got it."

"My bouquet is going to be made entirely from flowers mentioned in Shakespeare's plays," Agnes went on. "I'm wearing a traditional Renaissance wedding gown, and our vows will be in Elizabethan-era English."

"Wow," said Didi. She didn't know what else to say.

"We sent out the most gorgeous invitations," Agnes went on. "Cut edges, you know, with vellum overlay. They were stunning. And I figured the stationer would do our place cards, too, but—" Here, Agnes lowered her voice to a near whisper. "The thing is, Didi, we've encountered a bit of a cash flow problem. Those invitations were a tad over budget, and so was the dress, and, well, pretty much everything. So we need to find a more economical option for what's left."

"Right," said Didi. She understood now why she'd been called in.

By the time she hung up with Agnes, Didi felt like she had a handle on what Agnes wanted. Agnes said that her wedding planner, Gigi, would be in touch soon to settle all the details. It would take time to do it well, Didi knew, but she was confident she could do a good job. And if it involved design work, it'd be fun, too.

That feeling of confidence lasted about four minutes, until her phone rang again. It was a number she didn't recognize.

"Hello?"

"Yes, hello—" It was a woman's voice. *"No! Not there! On the porte-manteau! Does that look like a porte-manteau to you?"*

Didi was sure it was a wrong number and was about to hang up when the woman said: "Excuse me for that, some people wouldn't know turn-of-the-century furniture if it hit them on the head." The woman barked a short laugh. "I'm Gigi Sterngarten. Agnes told me to connect with you regarding place cards."

"Oh," said Didi, understanding it was the wedding planner. "Yes, hello. I just spoke with—"

"I'll be honest with you, I'm not thrilled she made this decision without my approval. I had someone lined up to do these cards, you know."

Didi's stomach clenched up. She didn't like to think she had stolen someone else's job.

"But, as I always say, brides must have what brides want," Gigi went on quickly. "I'm sorry, is this some kind of joke?"

"Umm, a joke?" Didi was confused.

"Not you," Gigi said. Her voice grew muffled, like she was pushing the phone away from her mouth. "This is not a *funeral*! This is a *wedding*! Get those flowers out of here!"

Didi did not know whom Gigi was talking to, but her heart went out to them.

"So, Didi, to recap, Agnes wants a bold, modern style. Abstract. Colorful." Didi was scribbling down her words. "Get me three designs by tomorrow at five. Text them to this number. I'll be in touch."

"Okay, yes, but I just—I have just one or two quick questions?" Didi ventured.

But Gigi didn't respond. Gigi, Didi realized, had hung up.

Didi had no idea how to get started with the designs—after all, what Gigi had described was the exact opposite of what Agnes had described. She spent a while experimenting in her sketchbook, then worked on her English essay, studied for her math test, and went to bed. She tossed and turned for much of the night.

In the morning, when she checked her phone, she saw she had a text from Gigi:

Nothing personal, but we're going in a different direction. Using computer. Your services no longer required.

I'm fired? Didi wondered. *How can I be fired? I haven't done anything yet.*

She was on the verge of tears when another text came through, also from Gigi:

Crossed signals. We will use your design. Send four mock-ups to me by noon today.

Noon? She'd said five P.M. before. And she'd asked for three designs, not four.

Before she could reply, another text popped up.

Make it five designs. We want options.

Didi's face felt hot with fury. It wasn't a sensation Didi felt often.

"Indira!" her mother called. "What is taking you so long? Breakfast is cold! You'll be late!"

Didi slid the phone into her backpack and pounded down the stairs to the kitchen, where her mother was waiting with two scrambled eggs and an English muffin. Her father was drinking a cup of coffee and reading his Sheila Orbacher book.

She stabbed at the eggs with her fork and tried to eat as quickly as she could.

"Did you finish the place cards?" Mrs. Singh asked, sitting down next to her.

Didi sighed. "I designed a few options for Gigi, but—"

"Gigi?" Mr. Singh looked perplexed. "I thought this was for Agnes."

"It is," Didi replied, chewing her eggs. "Gigi is the wedding planner. And she's a nightmare."

"Indira," her mother rebuked her. "Be charitable."

"I was," said Didi with her mouth full of English muffin. "I had something way worse to say."

Her mother didn't reply, just gave her the trademarked Singh stare, which said plenty, no words necessary.

"You know what Sheila Orbacher says, don't you?" asked her father.

"No," said Didi. She had a feeling she was going to find out.

"The customer may not always be right," said her father with a smile, "but they are always the customer."

That didn't clear things up much.

"Indira." Her mother leaned over the table toward her. "I am sorry this planner is being so challenging."

"Thanks, Maa."

"But do not forget that Agnes is a close friend of

the family, and your aunt and uncle will be at that wedding, with the triplets."

"I know, Maa," Didi replied. She didn't forget it for a second.

"You must do your best to give Agnes what she is paying for," said Mrs. Singh. Then she wrapped the remaining English muffin in a paper towel and handed it to Didi. "Take it to go! Or you'll be late!"

Didi rushed to homeroom and couldn't check her phone after that, as per school policy. She didn't have time to reply to Gigi until lunch, and by then, there were four more texts asking why she hadn't sent the designs?

Didi retreated to the lobby of her school, the only place where students were permitted to be on their phones in cases of emergencies. Even though she thought it was outrageous that Gigi could change the deadline like that, with no notice, she told her she'd have the designs in an hour.

Instead of heading to the cafeteria from there,

Didi walked up to the art room, where she could work without being disturbed. It was a good plan until, about halfway through lunch, Harriet breezed in with Amelia and Resa behind her.

"Aha!" Harriet pointed to Didi, then, turning to the others, said, "Told you she'd be here!"

"Harriet, you're not even supposed to be in this room," Resa warned. "You know you've been banned for life."

"Shhhh!" Harriet whispered. "Don't let anyone hear you."

"There's no one in here besides Didi," Resa said. "And besides, I think Mr. Ewoja will remember since he's the one who banned you."

"You pour *one* tub of glitter on your head . . . ," Harriet moaned.

"What are you up to, Didi?" Amelia walked over to where Didi sat and peered at the sketches laid out in front of her.

Didi sighed. "I have to send some designs to Agnes's wedding planner, but, honestly, I don't really like any of them and she wants lots of options."

Resa and Harriet crowded around the table to look.

"These," Resa concluded definitely, pointing to the sleek, modern ones. Resa was a fan of simplicity and minimalism. Her wardrobe choices proved that. You could bet your bottom dollar you'd find her in comfortable jeans paired with a white tank top and a colorful cardigan over that. If it's not broken, don't fix it was Resa's motto.

"No, those are too boring," Harriet weighed in. "Send these!" She pointed to the three most complicated, colorful designs, with little borders of stars and flowers and fireworks. Harriet's motto was: Go big or go home.

"What do you think?" Didi asked Amelia. "Which ones say 'modern and abstract and Shakespearean and dramatic' to you?"

Amelia raised her eyebrows at Didi. "Ummm, I don't think one design can say all those things. It's hard enough for one *person* to say all those things. How can you be Shakespearean and modern at the same time?"

Didi removed her eyeglasses and dropped her head into her hands. "I don't know! It's impossible!"

"Just send them all." Amelia shrugged. "She wanted options. Give her options."

Something buzzed inside Resa's jeans pocket. She pulled out her phone, looked at the number, and said: "Oooh, I gotta take this."

"Resa, you're not supposed to—" Didi started. Mr. Ewoja would be back from the bathroom soon, and he wouldn't be happy to see a student on the phone.

"I'm going to the lobby!" Resa assured her friend as she swiped the screen to answer the call. "Hi,

Mrs. Kim," she said. Didi could hear Mrs. Kim yelling.

"I know Alfie was upset," Resa replied. "Can I just . . . can I explain—"

As Resa disappeared down the staircase to the school's lobby, Didi turned to the others with a quizzical look.

"Remember her plan to make tons of money coaching tennis players?" Amelia said. "Well, that was the mother of one of her clients. Alfie Kim? He's in third grade, I think."

"He will not be returning for another lesson," said Harriet. "She had him doing laps, you know, to warm up, and he whined about it. She told him if he was gonna be a baby, he should take tennis lessons at the nursery school."

Didi winced.

"I warned her." Amelia shook her head.

Harriet had wandered over to Mr. Ewoja's recycled-art station, where he kept buckets of interesting, discarded items he thought his students could use to build sculptures. Harriet was rifling through the buckets, like she was on the hunt for something.

"Harriet, Mr. Ewoja has a whole system to organize those," Didi warned.

"Don't worry." Harriet picked up an old newspaper and unfolded it. "I'll put everything back where I found it."

Didi doubted that very much. She'd been in Harriet's bedroom. It was a level of mess she'd never even imagined. It looked like a giant had taken the whole room, shaken it up, and put it back down again.

"Oooh, look!" Harriet called to Amelia. "It's one of your mom's articles! About the unveiling of the new gazebo in the park."

"Yeah, that was from last week, I think." Amelia got a glint in her eye. "Hey, where do you all get the news, anyway? Social media, right? Or notifications from a news app?"

Didi had a sneaking suspicion Amelia wasn't just making conversation.

"Does this have anything to do with your mysterious business idea?" asked Didi.

"Maaaaaybe," said Amelia enigmatically. "But that's all I can say for now."

"I, for one, would never read a *paper* newspaper," said Harriet, scrunching up her nose and looking at her fingertips in disgust. "It gets your fingers *filthy* with smudges!"

"But how can you read the news online?" asked Amelia. "You don't have a phone."

"That is true," said Harriet, who was elbow-deep in the wood bucket now. "But I do have a brain, which is oh-so-resourceful."

"The *most* resourceful," Didi agreed.

"These wood chunks are the perfect size for my

skink chew toy," Harriet said, reaching her arm way, way into the bucket. "I've been looking for something—oooh, this!"

Her hand shot in the air. It was clutching a piece of wood.

"Bingo!" she exclaimed triumphantly. "You don't think Mr. Ewoja would mind if I borrowed this, right?"

"Uh, Harriet?" Didi tried to warn her friend that someone had walked through the door behind her.

"I think Mr. Ewoja *would* mind," answered Mr. Ewoja.

Harriet's face turned pale, and she dropped the wood back into the bucket then hurried to the doorway.

"Sorry, Mr. Ewoja," she said. "I was just—you know how it is when you get that artistic urge, right?"

"Uh-huh," Mr. Ewoja replied. His arms were crossed, and his face wasn't moving.

"Didi, I'm just gonna—I have to . . . my backpack! I left it in the cafeteria!" Harriet said in a rush. "Gotta run!"

Amelia leaned over and whispered to Didi: "That must have been some glitter accident."

"You have no idea," Didi replied.

It was tight, but Didi managed to finish up the five designs before lunch ended. She snapped photos and texted them to Gigi, just as Mr. Ewoja's room filled with boisterous eighth graders. Even though she raced down the stairs to social studies, she still ended up late. The relief she felt at having finished, though, was worth it. She just hoped Gigi would find at least one design she liked.

After school, she had a yearbook meeting. She was distracted the whole time, wondering if Gigi had responded about her designs. When the meeting was over, she was the first one out of the school. It was with equal parts excitement and dread that she powered up her phone, and within seconds, she was bombarded by a flurry of texts, accompanied by dings! and bings!

It came as no surprise they were all from Gigi. Didi dropped onto the metal bench in front of the school and waded through the flood of texts.

"You're popular today."

Didi looked up to see Val standing next to her. Val gave a little goodbye wave to the rest of the student government leaders, whom she'd been meeting with in the auditorium.

"Popular?" repeated Didi.

"All the texts?" said Val. She flashed Didi a smile almost as bright as her glittering T-shirt, which featured a sequined palm tree. The green of the tree matched her eyes, which were friendly enough but always seemed to possess a sly sparkle, too.

Resa couldn't stand Val, but Didi figured that was because they were so similar—ambitious, competitive, determined. Neither of them would give up without a fight, so, naturally, when they got together, there was a lot of fighting. Didi didn't mind Val. In fact, she thought she was fun to be around and full of good ideas . . . even if she did take those ideas too far sometimes.

"Oh, I'm not popular. Just pestered," said Didi glumly. "They're all from the same person. My boss."

"Don't tell me you're giving tennis lessons, too?" asked Val. "Because that doesn't sound like it's going so well for Resa."

"You heard about that, huh?"

"Yeah, Clyde McGovern's little brother just had a coaching session with Resa," said Val as she sat down next to Didi. "And he got so frustrated he broke his racket in half."

"Oh, no."

"Oh, yes."

"Well, I'm not coaching," said Didi, pushing her glasses up with her forefinger. "I'm designing place cards for this woman's wedding—Agnes Stein, you know her?"

"Of course," said Val. "Juliet with the broken leg instead of the broken heart."

"She didn't actually break her leg," said Didi. "But yeah, that one."

She sighed. "She's really nice, but her wedding planner is impossible! I sent her a ton of design options, and look what the planner wrote back." She handed her phone to Val.

"Wrong! All wrong!" Val read aloud. "Ouch. That's harsh."

"That's the tip of the iceberg," said Didi.

Val read on: "I clearly said these place cards should be baroque byzantine meets art nouveau! This is more beaux arts meets arts and crafts!"

Val looked up at Didi. "What is this lady even talking about?"

"Who knows?" Didi leaned back against the wall and closed her eyes. "And she's wrong—she never told me she wanted baroque anything before."

"Oh boy," Val kept reading. "She wants five more options by five P.M."

Didi moaned: "And it's already four thirty."

Didi was blessed with natural equanimity, and it took a lot to rattle her, but she was starting to feel seriously overwhelmed. "There's no way I can do it. I'll have to quit. I mean, I never quit, but I have to—what else can I do?"

Val narrowed her eyes. "How much are they paying you?"

"Fifty dollars," said Didi.

"Okay." Val nodded quickly. "It's a good thing you called me."

"I didn't actually call—"

"Here's what you do." Val handed the phone back to Didi. "Text this lady right now, and tell her that before you go *any* further, you need to get a few things straight." She nodded at Didi. "Text now. Go ahead."

"I don't know—" Didi started.

"Trust me," said Val. "This is my specialty."

"Negotiating with nightmare wedding planners is your specialty?" asked Didi, attempting a joke.

"Negotiating in general," said Val. "Also rhythmic gymnastics. And student government. Classical guitar, too. And I dabble in watercolors."

Didi grinned. Val was intense, but she was pretty good company. And Didi did trust her.

"So lemme see if I have this right—" Val pulled a bag of mixed nuts out of her backpack. She opened it and popped a peanut into her mouth. "You created five designs, and she rejected all of them, and now she wants five new ones?"

"Yep," said Didi. "Exactly."

Val was shaking her head. "No."

"No to what part?" Didi was confused.

"No to you being a dog chasing your own tail." Val crunched on a cashew. "What's stopping her from rejecting these five designs and making you do five more? Or ten more?"

Didi sighed. "I know."

"Here's what you're gonna do." Val ate an almond and considered. "Tell her, for the price you agreed on, you'll do three new designs, based on her feedback on the last round."

Didi was typing as Val spoke, trying to phrase her text exactly as Val dictated it.

"She has to pick one of those designs or else she

needs to pay more." She offered the snack bag to Didi. "Want a nut?"

"Uh, no, I'm good," Didi replied, finishing up the text. She looked up at Val and bit her lower lip. "But what if she gets angry?"

Val threw a handful of nuts into her mouth and chewed with gusto.

"She's already angry," she pointed out with her mouth full. "So you have nothing to lose."

She leaned over to read what Didi had written, and then, before Didi could stop her, she hit Send.

"Done!" Val announced. She patted Didi on the back, like a preschool teacher encouraging her tiny pupil.

"There," she said, smiling broadly. "That wasn't so bad now, was it?"

"Too early to tell," said Didi, with a nervous laugh.

The next morning, Val had only just arrived at home-room, and hadn't yet assumed her usual position at Ms. Davis's desk, when Didi walked in, feeling like a million bucks. She was wearing one of her favorite outfits—a long forest-green skirt, dotted with little yellow daisies, and a bright yellow shirt with fluttery sleeves. She'd pulled back her hair into a low, loose braid and slipped on silver hoop earrings.

"You seem a lot happier than the last time I saw you," said Val. She tossed her backpack onto her seat, then unzipped it and pulled out a package of brand-new purple pencils.

"I am," said Didi with a wide grin. "I have to thank you. Your text worked like a charm."

There was a pounding of footsteps, and then Resa rushed into the room. Every morning, Resa tried to beat Val to homeroom, and every morning, she failed, which made her feel like she was perpetually coming in second.

Now, seeing it was too late, she slowed her pace and ambled over to Didi, giving Val a suspicious look. Didi was her oldest and dearest friend, and she could sometimes be possessive of her, especially when Val was involved. "What are we talking about here? What worked like a charm?"

Val took the pencils to Ms. Davis's desk, where she began inserting them, one at a time, into the electric pencil sharpener.

"Oh, Val gave me some advice yesterday about dealing with that nightmare wedding planner," Didi explained.

"Really?" asked Resa. Didi could detect an edge to her voice.

"So what did Gigi say?" Val spoke loudly to be heard over the noise of the sharpener.

"Last night, I sent her the new designs, and she picked one, finally," said Didi. "So we're good. I can finish up now!"

"Awesome," said Val, dropping the sharpened pencils into Ms. Davis's pencil cup.

"Did you just seriously bring Ms. Davis a whole batch of pencils from home?" Resa asked, her arms crossed in front of her chest.

Val shrugged. "She was running low. And purple is her favorite color."

Resa hooked her arm into Didi's elbow and led her back toward their table.

"Since when are you best friends with Val?" Resa whispered.

Didi gave her friend a "Really, Resa?" look. "You're kidding, right?"

"I just mean, you could've called me to help you deal with that lady yesterday." A buzzing emanated from Resa's backpack. She glanced up to make sure Ms. Davis wasn't looking, then slipped her phone out and scanned the screen quickly.

"Ugh, it's Mrs. McGovern," Resa groaned as she powered the phone off and slipped it into her backpack. "She wants me to pay for the racket Clyde's brother broke. Like it's *my* fault the kid has no self-control!"

Amelia, who'd just walked in, tossed her backpack onto the table and sat down next to Didi.

"Yeah, I heard about that," she said. "Mrs. McGovern is one unhappy camper. She called my mom and told her she should write an article about the dangers of hiring unlicensed tennis instructors."

Resa looked aghast. "Your mom's not going to write it, is she?"

Amelia laughed. "Uhhh, no. That's not news." She turned to Didi. "So what did Gigi say about the designs?"

"Did you talk to *everyone* about this?" Resa said. "Except for me?"

"You're so busy with tennis stuff," Didi said, pushing a stray hair back behind her ear. "I didn't want to bother you." She turned to Amelia. "I had to put my foot down, but she finally picked a design—the one that looked really Shakespearean, with the first letter of the name really big and curly. So now all I have to do is buy the paper and write the names."

"You have to handwrite every name? You can't just print it out?" asked Resa.

Didi laughed. "Nope. These kinds of fancy parties like to have stuff done by hand." She shrugged. "But there's only fifty guests—just Agnes's and Rick's family and the theater troupe, so it's not too bad."

"Resa!"

Resa, startled, spun to face Clyde McGovern, who had walked into homeroom with a flock of friends behind him. "I heard your tennis-coaching business is really blowing up. As in, exploding."

"Funny," said Resa. "I heard the same thing about your—"

"Yes, Teresa?" Ms. Davis called. With her hawk eyes and cat ears, she never missed anyone stepping even a toe out of line. "Kindly finish your sentence. I'd love to hear."

Resa shot her eyes over at Clyde and then looked back at Ms. Davis. "Uhhh, you know, I can't remember what I was going to say now."

"That's a shame," Ms. Davis said. "Clyde, over here. Now."

"Ignore him," Amelia told Resa with a little shake of her head. "You know he's the worst."

The bell rang then, signaling the start of the school day. As the girls grabbed their backpacks, Didi turned to Resa and Amelia. "Anyone want to come to Paper Hub after school? I've gotta pick out fancy paper for the place cards."

"I totally would," said Amelia, "but I've got . . . a thing."

"Lemme guess," said Resa. "Your mystery project again?"

Amelia shrugged, noncommittal.

"Sorry, Di," Resa replied, "but I can't. I have a client."

Amelia and Didi exchanged skeptical looks. "Who's your victim this time?" asked Amelia.

Resa frowned. "Very funny."

The girls walked into the hallway, nearly colliding with Harriet, who was rushing in.

"I'm here!" Harriet exclaimed. "Did I miss anything?"

Didi laughed. "No more than usual."

"Hey, Resa," Harriet called as Resa turned, en route to math. "Larry's excited for his tennis lesson today! Go easy on him, would you? He's terrible at ball sports."

Amelia smiled at Didi. "What could possibly go wrong?"

Nobody was free to go to Paper Hub after school with Didi, but she didn't mind. Paper Hub was Didi's happy place. She could easily spend a whole afternoon there, testing colored gel pens, checking out the tiny erasers from Japan shaped like animals, and pining for the gigantic acrylic paint set. A big chunk of her allowance went into Paper Hub's cash register every week.

Gigi had instructed her to use a "muted yet resplendent cream card stock." She had no idea what that meant, really, but she hoped she'd know it when she saw it. She did not. She'd been staring at the same six pieces of beige paper for what seemed like ages when the bell hanging off the front door jingled.

Didi glanced up at the customer walking in and was nearly blinded by a flash of light. She blinked, and when she opened her eyes, she saw Val walking toward her, her trademark sequin shirt sparkling extra brightly.

"Didi!" Val exclaimed. "What are you doing at my favorite paper shop?"

"I love this place," Didi replied. "I come here all the time."

"I can confirm that," said the salesman, Hank, from behind the register. "You two are some of my best customers."

"When you're the class president, you have a *lot* of stationery needs," Val said. "And I'm starting my campaign for reelection, so I came for poster board. My usual order please, Hank!"

"No problem," Hank said. "Do you want to restock on glitter glue, too?"

"You know it." Val flashed him a smile, then turned to Didi. "What are you doing here?"

"I'm looking for paper for those place cards, actually," said Didi. She spread out the beige card stock she was holding. "Do these look muted yet resplendent?"

"Muted, yes. Resplendent, no way." Val tilted her

head. "What's the theme of the wedding? Can you show me the design?"

"The theme is Shakespeare, and they are *big* on drama." Didi turned on her phone and scrolled through her photos to find the photo she'd snapped. "Here's the final design."

Val turned to the wall of card stock, scanning for better options.

"So they definitely want something exciting." She pinched a bloodred card stock between her fingers and handed it to Didi. "Red's dramatic."

"Yeah, but most ink doesn't show up on dark paper," said Didi. "Plus, Gigi specifically asked for cream tones."

Val grabbed the paper from Didi's hands and laid it down on the counter. Then she turned to face Didi. "We need to brainstorm."

"We do?" Didi wasn't sure about this.

"Definitely. And lucky for you, I am pretty much the best brainstormer in this town. Probably this state. Possibly"—she raised her eyebrows—"this country."

Didi had no idea how to respond to this. She opted for, "Cool."

"Okay, so I'm going to ask you a series of questions," said Val, "and you have to respond as fast as you can. Got it? No thinking, just talking."

Didi's approach to life was a lot of thinking, little talking, so this did not seem like a plan she wanted to participate in. But Val was already grabbing her shoulders and locking eyes with her.

"When you hear 'Shakespeare,'" Val asked, "what do you see?"

"A book?"

"And?" prompted Val. "Just shout out words, don't stop! Stream of consciousness!"

"Ummm, goblets," Didi said. Val was making the "keep it coming" gesture, so Didi went on. "Velvet dresses, and wigs, and, um, swords? And wooden stages!" Val kept beckoning, so Didi kept talking. "So, I guess, ink, quills, and scrolls, and—"

Val held out her hand, her five fingers spread apart.

"That's it." She walked over to Hank, who'd returned to the register with a big batch of poster board. "Do you have any rolls of paper? Heavyweight? Cream-colored?"

"I think so, in the back," Hank said. "Let me get it."

"What are you doing?" asked Didi.

"Scrolls!" announced Val. "Each place card can be a little tiny scroll!"

"I don't know," said Didi. It was really different from what she originally had in mind. "It might be too out there."

"Come on, Didi!" Val's green eyes were sparkling. "Out there is *exactly* where you want to be! Out there is unique! One of a kind!"

"Maybe." The scrolls did sound very Shake-spearean, Didi thought, and Agnes had wanted drama. "I could write their names on the front, and then you'd unroll it to find out the table number—that could work, I think."

Val nodded. "And you could tie each with a little red ribbon!"

Hank brought out a large roll of beautiful paper that was just the right color and could be cut into pieces just the right size. And it cost even less than the paper Didi had been looking at. Gigi had said she'd reimburse Didi for the cost of the paper and calligraphy pens, but Gigi's budget was pretty tight. If Didi bought the more expensive card stock, she wouldn't have money for new, high-quality pens, which would make her work much better. Not only were the scrolls a cute idea, they'd cut costs so she could get pens. Win-win.

"This is really perfect," Didi said to Val. "Thank you so much."

"My brainstorming process never fails me," Val said, throwing her hands open in a "What can I say?" gesture. "But, Didi, how are you going to display the table numbers? You know, in the middle of the tables?"

Didi shrugged. "I'm not doing those." She paused. "I don't think I am, anyway."

"Well, you should," Val said. "You could charge an extra fee if you did."

"I don't know." Didi was just happy to have solved one problem. She didn't really want to open a whole new can of worms.

Val walked over to the register to pay for her big bag of supplies.

"Don't doubt yourself, Didi," she said. "As Willy himself said, 'to thine own self be true.'"

"Thanks," Didi said. But what she was thinking was, *If I'm being true to myself, I'd leave well enough alone.*

A few minutes later, as Didi was walking out of the store, a display in the crafts section caught her eye. Someone at the store had built a little cottage out of Popsicle sticks—but the sticks were dark and covered in a shiny gloss so they looked polished and professional, like real wood, the kind you use for furniture and floors . . . and stages. The beginnings of an idea percolated in Didi's brain.

"These are really cool," Didi told Hank, running her fingers over the cottage wall. "Do you sell sticks like this?"

"Sure, those are part of our collection of high-end crafting sticks," Hank replied. "Want to take a few samples home? I have a bunch of extra ones lying around in the back."

Didi smiled. "Definitely."

"Indira!"

Didi turned to face her mother, standing in the doorway. She hadn't heard her come in, but then again, the music was pretty loud. Didi liked to rock out when she was making art. It made her feel like she was going somewhere far away in her mind.

Her mother was miming covering her ears, which Didi knew by now was her "Turn down this racket" gesture. She paused the song on her phone.

"Finally!" Her mother's shoulders relaxed. "I've been calling and calling. Dinner will be ready in five minutes."

"Okay, thanks," said Didi. "Want me to set the table?"

"No, I've already done it," said her mom, walking over to her desk. "What are you working on all this time?"

"It's for Agnes's wedding." Didi stretched back in her chair, extending her arms up straight. She felt stiff from sitting in one position for so long. As soon as she'd gotten home from Paper Hub, she'd immediately set to work, and now the fruit of her labor sat before her on the desk. It was perfect.

"What is it?" Mrs. Singh asked.

"Well, I'm doing the place cards that'll have the table numbers on them," Didi said. "And I had an inspiration for how to display the table numbers— you know, in the middle of the table?"

Her mother picked up the creation and brought it closer for a better look. "A stage?"

Didi had taken the dark wood crafting sticks and glued them onto a small piece of cardboard, side by side, to form the stage floor. Then she'd made curtains, open, on either side of the stage, from a piece of red velvet she'd found in her fabric scrap box. Finally, in between the curtains, she'd mounted a piece of cream paper with the words *Table 1* written in Didi's careful calligraphy. It was a perfect miniature stage.

"Indira," her mother said, "it is beautiful."

"You think so?" asked Didi.

"Agnes will love this." Her mother set the center-piece carefully on the desk again. "You must take a photo and send it to her right now."

"Or maybe I should ask the wedding planner?" Didi wondered. "I don't want to bother the bride."

Mrs. Singh dismissed her worry with a wave. "That bad-tempered woman will say no. Talk to Agnes. She will love it."

She kissed the top of Didi's head. "Just as I said, you are a genius."

Mrs. Singh walked toward the door.

"Dinner is coming out of the oven now," she said. "You should send her a picture ASAP!"

"I will," Didi agreed.

"ASAP!" Her mother wagged her finger at Didi, in a feigned stern tone. "As! Soon! As! Possible!"

Didi laughed. "I'll send it now."

Didi didn't mind admitting it—her mom had been right. Val had been right, too, for that matter. Agnes loved the stage centerpieces. In fact, love was too gentle a word for the level of affection she showed.

MAGNIFICENT! her text read. And then, a few seconds later, another text followed: *MUST MUST MUST HAVE THESE!* Followed by: *Didi! Your mom was right! You're a genius!*

Didi knew it would take her a long time to make the four remaining centerpieces, but she was okay with that. They really were just right for a Shakespeare wedding.

When Gigi found out about the centerpieces, she was, predictably, not happy.

Agnes filled me in on the centerpieces, she texted Didi the next morning. *In the future, I am your point person! Do not contact Agnes directly!*

But, Didi noted, Gigi did not tell her to stop making them. After all, the bride must get what the bride wants. She'd said so herself. Armed with the knowledge that Agnes desperately wanted the stages, Didi stood her ground about her price. Forty dollars for the labor, plus the twenty-five dollars it cost for the high-end crafting sticks. It was definitely a reasonable price—and she told Gigi this.

After school, she stopped by Paper Hub for the crafting sticks and some other supplies, and when she got home, she finished about half of the place cards. By the time she got ready for bed, Didi felt really good about her burgeoning business. She was brushing her teeth while listening to her favorite song at a volume her mother would probably complain about later.

The song suddenly changed to "Here Comes the Bride!" Didi leaned over the sink and spit out her toothpaste. She didn't need to look at the phone to know who it was. She'd programmed that song to ring when Agnes called.

Didi's heart sank. Agnes had changed her mind, she was sure. She'd decided the centerpieces were too expensive, and then what would Didi do? She'd already paid for the materials.

She was tempted to just let the call go to voice mail, but she screwed her courage to its sticking place and swiped across the screen to pick up the call.

"Didi!" Agnes exclaimed. "Thank goodness you picked up!"

"What's up?" Didi ventured. "Is there an issue with the centerpieces?"

"The centerpieces?" Agnes sounded confused. "No, no, nothing like that. We have a huge problem. A disastrous, epic problem."

Didi's mind raced to guess what she could have done. "What is it?"

"It's Gigi!" Agnes all but yelled. "She's got mono!"

Didi was still processing that the problem had nothing to do with her. "Mono?"

"Yes—her doctor said she needs to rest for the next month!" Agnes was beside herself. "And the wedding is a week from tomorrow. One week!"

"Oh, no." Didi felt guilty at her relief. She wasn't happy Gigi was sick, but she was happy she wasn't to blame. "I'm really sorry. That's terrible."

"It is terrible!" Agnes cried. "It's catastrophic!"

Didi could see why Agnes had chosen a career in the theater. She certainly had a natural flair for the dramatic. "But I'm sure you'll figure it out. If you need any help, just let me know."

"Well," said Agnes, "I'm glad you said that. I do need your help."

"Okay," Didi replied. "What can I do?"

"You, genius girl, can take Gigi's place!"

"Huh?" That was all Didi could muster in her amazement.

"I want you to be the substitute wedding planner!" Agnes clarified.

Didi was speechless.

"Didi?" asked Agnes. "Are you there?"

"Yeah," Didi replied.

"Yeah, you'll do it?" Agnes sounded relieved.

"Yeah, I'm here," replied Didi. "The wedding planning . . . I guess . . . well, I have some questions."

That was putting it mildly.

Didi usually looked forward to sleeping in on Saturdays, but the next morning, she was up bright and early. She tried to go back to sleep, but she was nervous and couldn't relax. So she got up and headed straight to her desk to finish the place cards—or the ones she could finish, at least. Agnes had told her there would probably be a few changes to the seating chart—which was just the sort of thing, Agnes said, that Didi would be great at handling.

Didi had told Agnes she needed to think about her proposal—but the truth was, she'd already made up her mind. It was so much—too much—and she'd gotten into this to make art. Wedding planning wasn't art—at least, not the kind she liked to make.

"Indira," called her mother from downstairs. "You have guests!"

She walked to the doorway of her bedroom in time to see Amelia and Resa stomping up the steps.

"Hey!" Didi was glad to see them. "What's up?"

"Will you please explain to Amelia over here"—Resa pointed her thumb in Amelia's direction—"that I am wonderful with kids!"

"Look, I didn't mean to insult you," Amelia interjected as they walked into Didi's room. Resa plopped down on Didi's perfectly made bed, flinging herself back against the pillow. She spent almost as much time at Didi's house as she did at her own—the two had been inseparable since kindergarten.

"It's not that you insulted me, it's that you're wrong!" Resa exclaimed. "The problem isn't my teaching! It's these clients! They're whiners! Babies! They have no discipline or stamina!"

"Did something else happen with the tennis lessons?" Didi hated being dragged into the middle of her friends' arguments, but it seemed inevitable when Resa and Amelia got together. They both looked to her for agreement, and she felt like she was the rope in a tug-of-war.

"It was Larry's fault!" Resa sat up on the bed, pulling her legs into crisscross applesauce position.

"But you said everything went great with Larry's lesson," Didi pointed out.

"Yeah, well." Resa looked sheepish. "Can you blame me for trying to keeping this stuff under wraps? It's bad publicity!"

"Too bad Larry doesn't share your discretion," said Amelia.

"He wasn't paying attention during his lesson! And Eleanor shouldn't have even been on the court! Who lets their girlfriend hang out next to them when they're in the middle of playing tennis? How is this my fault?"

Didi sank into her desk chair. "What happened?"

"We were in the middle of a lesson and I waited—I waited a few minutes for him to wrap up his conversation, but, seriously, it was taking forever, so I served. It was a perfect serve, by the way, bull's-eye, but he was so busy looking at Eleanor he didn't hit the ball."

"Instead, the ball hit him," said Amelia.

"Which wasn't even the problem, because it hit him in the arm—no big deal—but then it ricocheted off his arm—"

"Those balls are bouncy," Amelia pointed out.

"And hit Eleanor," said Resa.

"In the face," Amelia elaborated.

Didi winced. "Ouch."

"She's fine!" Resa hastened to add. "It's just that her glasses broke."

"So Larry walked out and refused to pay the fee," Amelia explained. "In fact, he wants Resa to help pay for Eleanor's new glasses."

"Which is preposterous!" Resa interjected.

"So I told Resa that maybe she needs to give the lessons a break," said Amelia. "And she doesn't want to."

"Well, it's good money!" Resa tugged at her stretchy orange headband. "It's thirty dollars an hour. If I do one lesson a day, that's $150 a week—just for weekdays!"

"Yeah, but half the people are demanding their money back," Amelia pointed out.

Resa narrowed her eyes at Amelia. "Do you have a better moneymaking idea?"

Amelia tucked her hair behind her ears and nodded. "Maybe. And I'm almost ready to tell you about it."

Resa flung her hands in the air in frustration. "We'll all be senior citizens by the time you perfect your amazing business idea."

"I, um, I have something," Didi piped up.

"Oh yeah?" Amelia looked up with interest. "What?"

"Okay, it sounds kind of nuts," warned Didi, "but Agnes wants me to be her new wedding planner."

Resa scrunched her eyebrows together. "But she already has a planner. Madam Text-a-Lot."

"Yeah, right, but Gigi has mono," said Didi. "And it turns out she's pretty much the only wedding planner in town."

"Really?" asked Amelia. "Ummm, that's a market need right there."

"But, Didi,"—Resa sat up straighter on the bed—"that's a lot of responsibility."

"I know." Didi nodded.

"I mean, it's a *wedding*," Resa went on. "One of the most important days in a person's life. And, plus, it's a huge production." She ticked off items on her fingers. "Flowers, music, food, cake, toasts, party favors."

"You know a lot about weddings," Amelia observed.

"My mom's a baker," Resa replied. "She made wedding cakes before she opened the doughnut shop. I helped."

"I mean, Gigi told her that everything is basically done—all those things you said, they're already picked out and set up," said Didi. "All I'd have to do is make sure they get delivered and put in the right place and stuff. And I'm good with organization."

"That you are," said Amelia.

"Sometimes I think you were born with a to-do list in your hand," Resa joked.

"Still," said Amelia.

"I mean, it's a great opportunity, but maybe, you know, you try it in a few years," said Resa.

"Right," agreed Didi. "Money's not everything."

"Wait a second," Resa said. "How much money are we talking about here?"

"Well, Agnes was paying Gigi in installments, and if I took over, Agnes said she'd pay the last installment to me instead of Gigi," Didi replied. "And that'd be five hundred."

Resa leaned forward. "Five hundred *dollars*?"

Didi nodded.

"*Didi!*" yelled Resa, scrambling off the bed and racing to Didi's side. "*You have* to do it!"

"But you said—"

"Forget what I said!" Resa was looking at Didi intently. "That's way too much money to turn down! And if you get stuck, we can always help you."

Didi chewed on her thumbnail. It was a bad habit she had since she was little, and, though she'd mostly stopped, it flared up again when she got stressed or nervous.

"What do you think?" Didi asked Amelia.

"I think with that kind of money, you could buy

yourself a subscription to PictureHouse for years," Amelia said.

"Didi," Resa urged, "call Agnes back right now and tell her yes! Yes! Absolutely yes!"

She squatted down next to Didi.

"You can do this, Didi," said Resa. "I know you can."

Didi nodded. "Okay."

But she wasn't so sure. She wasn't sure at all.

"Didi!" Harriet's voice broke through Didi's wall of concentration. "Earth to Didi!"

"Yeah?" Didi looked up from the overstuffed accordion folder on which she was focused. The folder, labeled STEIN/CHAN WEDDING, took up the space where her lunch bag should have been on the cafeteria table.

"Aren't you going to eat?" asked Harriet.

Harriet's dark hair had been pulled into a high ponytail with a large green scrunchie. She wore a matching green T-shirt with a gigantic giraffe head on the front. From her earlobes dangled earrings in the shape of zebras. Harriet liked to select outfits according to theme, and today's theme, Didi could tell, was safari.

"Lunch's half over," Harriet reminded her.

"I just have a lot to do for Agnes's wedding," Didi explained. The wedding was only five days away. She didn't see how she was going to squeeze lunch in . . . or dinner . . . or breakfast, either.

"You're a workaholic!" Harriet wagged her plastic fork at Didi.

Didi scrutinized a receipt. "Someone ripped the top part so I can't tell where this is from! Is it for flowers? Or catering? Or something else?"

"What's the matter?" asked Resa, who sat across from Didi and was enjoying a chicken-salad sandwich on crunchy French bread. Resa always had the best lunches, courtesy of her mom, who owned the town's hottest doughnut shop and had spent many years catering. "I thought Gigi took care of everything."

Didi snorted. "All Gigi took care of was making a total mess out of everything!" She pulled a handful of papers out of the folder. "Look at this! Nothing's organized. Half of it is impossible to read. I don't know what she's already paid for or when deliveries are supposed to happen or anything."

Amelia, sitting next to Didi, leaned over and closed Didi's accordion folder with both hands.

"Break time," she said, taking the folder away and clearing a space for Didi's lunch.

"Just leave me the seating chart!" Didi pleaded. "I can work on it while I eat."

Amelia shook her head firmly. "You'll burn out if you don't recharge."

Reluctantly, Didi opened her lunch bag and unscrewed the top of the thermos. Her mom had packed leftover spaghetti. That was some consolation. The world always looked brighter after spaghetti.

"Ooooh," said Harriet. "I am seriously in the mood for spaghetti. I should make some tonight. Eleanor's coming over, and she could use some cheering up."

"What's wrong with Eleanor?" asked Amelia.

Resa suddenly appeared to be incredibly engrossed by her lunch. Her eyes were glued to the sandwich.

"She's been down in the dumps," Harriet replied, looking pointedly at Resa. "Ever since . . . the *incident*."

Resa, unable to stand it anymore, spun to face Harriet. "Her glasses broke! It's not the end of the world! I didn't poke her eye out!" she exclaimed. "Besides, I *said*, 'Heads-up!' How is it my fault that she wasn't paying attention?"

"If you say so." Harriet gave an exaggerated shrug.

"I already shut down the business, okay?" said Resa. "What else do you want me to do?"

"You did?" Amelia asked, surprised.

Didi was twisting forkfuls of spaghetti and eating them as fast as she could so she could get back to work.

"I'm sure you could improve your teaching if you wanted to," said Didi encouragingly. "It just takes practice, like everything."

"Yeah, I guess, but it was kind of ruining tennis for me," said Resa. "I mean, I love tennis so much, but I guess I don't love teaching it."

Amelia pursed her lips together and said a lot by saying nothing.

Resa rolled her eyes. "Go ahead and say it."

"Say what?" asked Amelia, her eyes wide.

"I can see you just itching to say, 'told you so,'" said Resa.

Amelia shrugged and took a big bite out of her peanut butter and jelly sandwich.

"But I was totally right that it's a great business idea," Resa said. "I had tons of customers and made plenty of money . . . or I would have if so many people hadn't asked for refunds."

"You could run the tennis-coaching business and just get other people to teach the lessons," suggested Amelia.

"Yeah," Resa sighed. "Maybe once the smoke clears."

"While we're on the subject of tragic endings . . ." Harriet paused, dramatically. "I have also shut down my business."

"What business?" asked Resa.

Harriet looked offended. "The skink-chew-toy business!"

"Ohhhhhh, right," said Amelia. "The chew toy didn't work out?"

"Oh no, the chew toy was perfect!" Harriet tossed a cheese puff into her mouth and munched cheerfully. "Zappa loves it! She's over the moon. It turns out I am a genius at designing chew toys!"

"Sooooooo . . . ," said Amelia. "What's the problem?"

"The world is not ready for my genius," said Harriet. "I could find only one person who wanted a toy—Gus, the guy who owns the sub shop way down at the end of Cashew Street."

"So, not a lot of skink owners around here, huh?" asked Didi. "Well, I know it's selfish, but I'm relieved to hear that. Those animals give me the creeps."

Resa looked over at Amelia. "Aren't you going to tell her, 'told you so'?"

Amelia took a gargantuan bite of her sandwich and said nothing.

Without anyone noticing, Didi started looking through her accordion folder again, on the hunt for a specific slip of paper.

"What about your big, secret idea?" Resa asked Amelia. "Whatever happened with that? We told you all the gory details about our businesses, so it's your turn—what are *you* working on?"

Amelia finished chewing her bite. "I'm alllllllmost ready to tell you. Promise."

"Didi." Harriet raised her eyebrows reprovingly. "I thought you were taking a break."

"I know, I know." Didi looked up with a guilty expression. "But I just remembered I was supposed to call the band to confirm their set list, and to do that, I need to find Gigi's notes, which were—oh! I think this might be it."

She pulled out a small scrap of paper with sloppy cursive scrawled across it. "No, this is the florist's number—which reminds me, shoot, they left me a message saying they can't get red peonies this time of year. Agnes *specifically* said she wanted red peonies—"

The bell rang, signaling the end of lunch. Didi had managed to take only a few bites of spaghetti and hadn't managed to make any sense of Gigi's folder. She had a yearbook meeting again after school, and then she had a whole other centerpiece to make for the wedding, plus a mountain of phone calls and emails to vendors. She also had a quiz in science and an essay in English to prepare for. She had no idea how she could possibly get it all done and sleep, too.

Seeing the look of panic that flickered across her friend's face, Resa helped put the papers back in the folder. "Don't worry, Di," she said with a smile. "Harriet and Amelia and I will totally be there on the wedding day to make sure everything goes smoothly. Like I told you before, we got your back."

"Thanks." Didi forced a smile in return, but the truth was that having the girls there at the wedding was just a tiny fraction of the help she needed. If she didn't get some serious backup immediately—ASAP, as her mother would say—there wouldn't be a wedding day.

Didi was in a groove. A gluing groove. She'd finished the floorboards for the last stage centerpiece, and now she was working on the curtains. It was like the pulsating music blaring out of her headphones was pumping new blood into her, giving her the energy she needed to power through.

"Indira!"

Didi was so startled to hear her mother's voice suddenly right next to her, she let out a full-blown scream.

Her mother's frown grew deeper. "You will wake your father!"

"Sorry, it's just—you scared me."

"Indira," her mother said, lifting the headphones off her neck. "Do you know what time it is?"

Didi glanced at the clock on her nightstand, but before she could reply, her mother went on: "Midnight! And you have school tomorrow!"

"I know, I just have so much to do!"

"Homework?"

"No, for Agnes's wedding," Didi said, resuming her gluing. She didn't have time to waste with chitchat. "I have to finish this centerpiece, and then I have to tackle the seating chart, and after that, I just have a few more emails to send off, but then I promise I am going to bed. It shouldn't take more than—" Didi yawned as she calculated her workload "—two hours or so."

Mrs. Singh did not move a muscle. Her face wore its expressionless stare, which Didi knew by now signaled profound disapproval.

"No," Mrs. Singh said flatly.

"No what?" asked Didi.

"No, you will not stay up until two o'clock in the morning on a school night, Indira," she said firmly. "School must come first."

"But then—" Didi felt herself flush with anger and worry. "I don't have a choice! The band canceled, so I have to find another one that's free Saturday and can play Renaissance music and doesn't cost a fortune. And also, the florist doesn't have any of the flowers Agnes wants—no daffodils, no peonies, no daisies. Like, any of them! I've called the Kings Hotel twelve times, and they won't pick up or call me back, and I'm pretty sure it's because Gigi never paid them, and I am pretty sure that if she didn't pay them, they gave away the date to someone else, which means *Agnes has no place to get married*!"

Didi hadn't stopped gluing, but in her state of agitation, she had glued the curtains in upside down. She realized this now and let out a strangled cry.

"Oh noooo!" she moaned, pulling the floorboards up and watching them drip glue onto her desk. "They're all—they're sticky now! Look what I did!"

Mrs. Singh had said nothing during Didi's rant. Now she sat down on the edge of Didi's bed, faced her daughter, and took both of Didi's hands in hers.

"The glue's gonna dry," Didi protested.

"Indira," her mom said, "look at me."

Didi lifted her brown eyes to meet her mother's, which were identical in color and full of compassion.

"*Beta*," Mrs. Singh said, "this is too much pressure for you."

"I should've never accepted the job," Didi said. "But what can I do? If I quit, Agnes will have no one! I can't be responsible for ruining her wedding!"

"You have made a commitment, and you must honor it," her mother said.

"Ohhhhkay, but you just said how it's too much pressure." Didi pulled her hands back and hunched over in her chair. "So which is it? What do you want me to do?"

"I said it is too much pressure for you," her mother clarified. "Just you. You can do it, but you must have help."

Didi gave her head a little shake. "Like who?"

"Like me!" Mrs. Singh stretched her hands out to her sides, presenting herself. "What am I? Chopped liver?"

This was one of her mom's favorite American expressions. It cracked Didi up every time.

"Linda's shop can get peonies and daisies," her mother said. "And Linda will give you a good discount, I am sure of it."

Didi looked up with surprise. "That could actually work."

"And I will glue these things for you, *beta*," she said. "It is not hard. I can do it."

"I don't know—"

But Mrs. Singh would not let her finish. Instead, she stood up, peeled the bedspread back from the perfectly made bed, and guided Didi gently into it by her shoulders. She pulled the covers up under her chin, then kissed her on the forehead.

"Now, you sleep," her mother instructed. "And tomorrow, when you go to school, you think about school. You can ask Resa and the other girls if they will help. I am sure they will. You help them all the time."

"Maybe," Didi murmured. Her eyelids felt so heavy she couldn't help but let them drop closed.

Her mother squeezed her hand for a long moment. By the time she let go, Didi was fast asleep.

Didi could not get out of bed the next morning. She kept hitting the snooze button on her alarm until finally her mother came in and told her she had only fifteen minutes before she needed to be out the door.

She threw on the first dress she saw, splashed some water on her face, and bolted out the door, but still, she arrived in homeroom after Resa and Amelia.

Resa was deep in conversation with Val when Didi rushed in, throwing her backpack onto the floor by her chair.

"Who is it?" Val was demanding. "Just tell me."

"Sworn to secrecy," Resa said. Then she mimed zipping her lips closed.

"Is it Clyde? Or Giovanni? Is it—" Val pursed her lips and squinted, looking like she was deeply pondering something. "Is it *Harriet*?"

"All I can tell you is, someone is planning to run

against you for class president," said Resa, shrugging. "That's all I'm at liberty to say."

Val's face turned nearly as red as her hair. She exhaled loudly, then spun around and headed to Ms. Davis's desk, where she retrieved an eraser to clean the whiteboard.

"Why are you torturing Val?" Amelia asked. "Why not just tell her you're running against her?"

"I want to retain the element of surprise," said Resa, grinning. Then turning to Didi, she asked: "Do I have your vote, Didi?"

Didi nodded.

"Didi, are you okay?" Amelia asked. "You look kind of tired."

Before Didi could reply, Harriet breezed in in a pair of fire-engine red leggings and a yellow tunic with red pinstripes. Her hair was in a jaunty side ponytail.

"Yes!" she exclaimed, pumping her fist in the air victoriously. "I still have three minutes of homeroom! This is a record for—" In the middle of her victory spin, she caught sight of Didi and gasped. "What happened?"

Didi felt her shoulders tense up defensively. "Nothing."

Harriet plopped down in the empty chair next to Didi.

"You're not wearing lip gloss. You always wear clear lip gloss."

"I don't always—"

"Your hair has not been brushed!" Harriet went on. "This is unheard of!"

"Oh, well, that's just silly—"

But Harriet was already putting her hand to Didi's forehead.

"You're not hot," she observed. "Describe your symptoms!"

"I'm just really tired," Didi said, shrinking back from Harriet's hand. "I stayed up really late working on wedding stuff."

"Didi." Resa laughed. "You need to stop being such a perfectionist. Everything's going to be fine. It'll work out."

"No, it won't," Didi said firmly.

"What do you mean?" asked Resa.

"I mean, I'm not being a perfectionist," Didi said. "It's just way too much for one person to do."

She remembered her mother's advice from the night before. It was true—Didi had been there to help Resa win the lemonade-stand contest because Resa had desperately wanted to win VIP passes to Adventure Central. She'd been there when Harriet needed to raise money to replace her brother's guitar, which she'd broken. And she'd been there for

Amelia when she'd arrived at a new school with no friends at all. Didi was always there for her friends, and it wasn't unreasonable to expect that they'd be there for her, too.

She looked from Harriet, who was panic-stricken, to Resa, who was confused, to Amelia, who offered a small smile.

"I need help," Didi finally said. "Will you help? Like, right away?"

There was a surprised silence.

"Absolutely!" Harriet exclaimed, throwing her arms around Didi.

"Of course," said Resa.

Amelia nodded.

The bell rang then, and the usual stampede toward the door began.

"So are we helping you *now* now? Because I'm up for that! I would love a reason to miss social studies for a while." Harriet had entered full scheming mode. "I'll say I'm having intestinal challenges. Or narcolepsy, maybe?"

Didi laughed and put a hand on Harriet's shoulder.

"It can wait until after school," she said. "I'll meet you out front."

Harriet looked sorely disappointed. "If you say so."

13

By four P.M., the girls were settled in around Didi's dining room table, eating hot, cheesy pizza. Amelia had arranged for a pie to be delivered from Napoli's Best—half plain for Didi and Amelia, half meat lovers with added pineapple for Resa and Harriet. Resa wasn't a fan of pineapple, but Harriet felt very strongly about it.

"Meat lovers pizza without pineapple is like a peanut butter and jelly sandwich without the bread!" she exclaimed. "It's an essential ingredient."

Resa had learned not to argue when Harriet

dug in her heels like this. She'd just pick off the pineapple.

Now they were all devouring their hot, cheesy, saucy goodness—all except Didi, who picked at the crust listlessly. Across the room, her beta fish swam in slow circles around his fishbowl, looking glum. She shared his sentiments.

"Okay, Didi, where do we start?" said Amelia, whose pizza slice was folded in half—or, as she called it, "city style."

Didi took off her glasses and rubbed her eyes.

"I don't even know," she said. "It's all such a mess."

"Okay, let's just go down the list," suggested Resa. She used a knife and fork to eat her slice, which was so overloaded with pepperoni and sausage and meatballs the crust underneath it threatened to tear. "First off, the venue. Anything left to do there?"

"Uhh, yeah," said Didi.

"Okay, what?" asked Resa.

"Well, for starters," said Didi, "we need a venue."

"Seriously?" asked Amelia. "How can Agnes get married this weekend if she doesn't have a place to get married?"

"She was supposed to get married at the Kings Hotel, but they just left me a voice mail saying they never got Agnes's deposit, so they released the date to someone else," explained Didi. "They said they called Gigi a bunch of times but she never called back."

"Typical Gigi!" Harriet smirked. She had eaten all the pineapple pieces and was now tearing off pieces of the slice and popping them into her mouth. This was not a neat way to consume pizza, and Didi kept passing her napkins in a subtle attempt to keep the situation under control.

"Okay," said Amelia, pulling a pencil from behind her ear and writing *Wedding To-Do List* on a fresh piece of loose-leaf paper. Underneath, she scribbled *Venue.* "What kind of a space does Agnes want?"

Didi pondered this. "Something available and something cheap."

"The weather's going to be stupendous all week," said Harriet. "How about a wedding alfresco? At the park! In the new gazebo!"

"We don't have time to get permits," Resa chimed in.

"Did you forget I know the guy who knows the guy?" Harriet winked. "I can pull some strings for you."

"Well," said Didi, mulling the proposition over. "I'd have to ask Agnes, and it'd mean a lot more work—we'd have to get tables, chairs, everything. But it could work, I guess."

"I'll take that as a resounding yes," said Harriet.

She peeled a piece of pepperoni off her slice and popped it into her mouth.

"Okay, next on the list," said Resa. "Do you have the food all set?"

"Uhh, not so much," Didi nibbled at her slice, which was growing cold.

"Meaning?" Resa asked.

"Meaning we have no food," said Didi. "The Kings Hotel was doing the catering, so the food fell through, too. And the cake."

"Well, the cake's one thing you don't have to worry about," said Resa. "My mom can do it."

"Are you sure?" asked Didi.

"Di," said Resa, "I've got you covered. But you'll have to figure food out. My mom's catering days are long gone."

"Well, you can't decide on food until you know where she's getting married," Harriet pointed out.

"Right," agreed Amelia. She was taking careful notes in her neat handwriting.

"Okay, what about music?" Resa said, eating a large forkful of spicy sausage. "Did you talk to the band about the set list?"

"The former band, you mean?" Didi replied. "They broke up a week ago. There is no band, so there is no set list."

"*Drama!*" yelled Harriet with a mouthful of pizza.

"Maybe they'll get back together?" asked Amelia hopefully.

"The singer eloped with the flute player," said Didi flatly.

"Awwww," cooed Harriet, "that's romantic. What's the matter with that?"

"The singer was engaged to the cornett player," said Didi.

"Ooooh, intrigue!" Harriet whistled. "What's a cornett player?"

"No idea." Didi shrugged. "But I'm guessing they are really hard to replace. I mean, how many bands do you know who play Renaissance music?" She took a bite of pizza and chewed gloomily.

Harriet gasped, and all three girls turned to look at her. "The Skinks! They can play at the wedding!"

Didi exchanged a look with Resa. She knew she had to proceed with caution. Harriet felt fiercely protective of her brothers and their band.

"You know I love the Skinks," said Didi emphatically, "but they definitely do not specialize in Renaissance music. They're a rock band."

"They've done every kind of music you can imagine!" Harriet leaned forward, her side ponytail grazing the pile of pizza pieces on her plate. "Heavy metal, kids' music, rock—they can do anything!"

"Sure, okay," Resa jumped in. "But none of them plays the flute or the cornett, whatever that even is."

"Will you just ask Agnes?" pleaded Harriet. "They could audition for her! Show her what they can do."

Didi knew the Radical Skinks, with their blue-haired fanatics, were not the right band for Agnes's Shakespeare wedding, but she also knew time was running out and any band that could carry a tune was probably better than no band at all.

"Okay, I'll ask her," said Didi. "But I am not promising anything."

Harriet lunged over the table to hug Didi. "You won't regret this!"

When she straightened up, the front of her shirt had a large pizza-colored splotch on it.

"Uh, Harriet?" Didi nodded in the direction of the stain and handed her a stack of Napoli's Best napkins.

"Okay," said Amelia, looking at her list. "What about flowers?"

"That was a disaster, but my mom's taking care of it," Didi replied. Her appetite was returning, so she took a large bite of her cold-but-still-delicious slice. "Linda's coming to the rescue."

"All right," said Amelia, looking up from her notepad. "Anything else? Please tell me she has a wedding dress?"

Didi laughed. "Yes, she does, and it's beautiful.

Long-sleeved, all lace, with this fairy-tale train that turns into a bustle for dancing."

Resa helped herself to another slice of pizza and was picking off the pineapple chunks. She looked up encouragingly at Didi. "Okay, great! See, Di? We've got this under control."

"So Harriet's going to ask her connection about the permit, and she's also dealing with the band," Amelia said. "You're going to have them prepare an audition of Renaissance music for Agnes, right?"

"Yes, ma'am!" said Harriet with a salute.

"Resa's got the cake, your mom's on flowers, and I'll research a few food options for an outdoor wedding," said Amelia.

"And I'll talk to Agnes and check in about everything," said Didi. She wiped her mouth with a napkin and leaned back in her chair. "Thanks for the pizza, Amelia. It was seriously amazing. I've never been to this place."

"You're welcome," said Amelia. "But it was on the house."

"Free pizza?" Harriet furrowed her eyebrows together. "Too good to be true. What's the catch?"

Amelia laughed. "Well, it's just a thank-you."

"For what?" asked Resa.

"Remember that business idea I had simmering?" Amelia asked. "It's cooked."

"You're starting a pizza parlor?" shrieked Harriet. "Yes! Genius! The world can never have too much pizza!"

Amelia grinned. "My business idea's a tad smaller than that."

"Well," said Resa, finishing off her slice. "Don't keep us in suspense."

"Okay," said Amelia, pushing her hair behind her ears. "So, a few weeks ago, my mom was telling me how the newspaper was trying to make more videos to put on their site. Everyone loves watching videos, right?" She sipped from her glass of water. "But the thing is, none of the writers have time to do more work, and they don't have the budget to pay new people just to make videos. So I thought, *I've* got some time. I care about local news, and I can put together a video on my phone in no time."

"So you're making videos for the paper?" asked Didi. "That's incredible!"

"Well, not yet," Amelia explained. "I mean, I'm making news videos, and if they take off, then maybe the paper will pay me to feature them. Eventually."

"So I'm confused," said Resa, wrinkling her brow. "What does this have to do with pizza?"

"I made my first video," Amelia said. "I interviewed some people on how they feel about the new gazebo—and I put in a sponsored bit at Napoli's Best. You know, basically a free ad. So, to thank me, they gave me a voucher for a free pizza."

"Win-win," Harriet said.

"Yeah." Amelia smiled. "For right now, I'm just trying to make enough videos so that it seems like I have a real channel, but if one of those videos goes viral—"

"You'll get a billion followers!" Harriet squealed.

"Right," said Amelia. "Well, maybe not a billion, but if I get even a couple of thousand followers, local businesses might pay to advertise in my videos."

"Pay you?" Resa was skeptical. "For ads? Really?"

"I know it sounds too good to be true, but

look—" Amelia pulled a stapled packet of paper out of her backpack. On the cover, it read *Business Plan*.

"You made a business plan?" asked Didi.

Amelia nodded. "My mom said she thought it would help me look legit in the eyes of the paper." She handed it to Didi. "I searched it online. It wasn't hard."

Didi flipped through the pages. There was a section on *Competition*, another on *Target Audience*, one on *Marketing*, and even a part called *Financial Projections*. It looked super organized and well researched, which was just how Amelia rolled.

"Basically, I'd have no competition, because no one else is making local news videos for people our age, and we get all our news from watching videos online, so there is definitely an audience," she explained. "Businesses that sell to us—the pizza place, the arcade, the ice-cream shop—they'll pay for ads if enough people watch."

"I'm in to help!" Harriet said, leaning back in her chair. "But I'll need hair and makeup provided to me."

Amelia laughed. "I'd love for you all to make the videos with me—when we're done with the wedding. Right now. Didi's the one who needs help."

"Who knew a wedding could be such a headache?" asked Didi.

"Probably every wedding planner everywhere." Resa laughed. "But, as Agnes would say, the show must go on."

"I'm in heaven!" Harriet exclaimed rapturously. "Paradise! Nirvana!"

She was staring, wide-eyed, at the rainbow assortment of small cakes on Resa's dining room table. It was Wednesday, and with only three days until the wedding, Mrs. Lopez had invited Agnes and Didi over for a cake tasting. When they were done, Resa had invited the rest of the girls over for leftover-cake tasting.

Amelia read the flavors from the little handwritten signs in front of each cake. "Butterscotch with caramel glaze, chocolate with Madagascar vanilla fondant, strawberry shortcake, carrot cake, and—" Amelia nodded approvingly "—this one looks cool. Death by Chocolate."

"If you've got to go, it's the best way." Resa grinned, sliding her knife into the Death by Chocolate cake. She gave the first slice to Harriet, who looked like she might faint from the excitement otherwise.

Harriet placed a forkful into her mouth. "This one," she said conclusively.

"It's the first one you tried." Didi smiled.

Harriet shrugged. "When you know, you know."

"Which one did Agnes choose?" asked Amelia.

"Chocolate with vanilla frosting," said Didi, digging into her cake slice for a little bite. "And instead of a three-layered cake, she's doing a cupcake pyramid. It looks so cool."

"Next!" said Harriet, holding her empty plate out to Resa.

As Resa cut her a slice of carrot cake, Amelia chimed in. "Oh, hey, what did Agnes think of the Skinks' audition?"

"*Loved* it!" Harriet interjected.

"Really?" asked Resa, forgetting to hide her surprise.

"They hit it out of the ballpark!" Harriet took a bite of the carrot cake. "Oh, *this* one, definitely!"

Didi laughed.

"The Skinks' audition wasn't anything like what Agnes had planned, but she was totally into it," said Didi. "They're going to play updated Renaissance songs—the same melody and lyrics but played on electric guitar and drums instead of flute and cornett. They're calling themselves the Renaissance Skinks."

"That actually sounds pretty cool," said Resa as she licked frosting off her fingers.

"So music's all set, and cake, too?" said Amelia.

"Yep, and Agnes spoke to my mom about flowers. She's getting peonies for her bouquet, but they were too expensive for centerpieces, so she's using white daisies, with some marigolds and tulips, for the tables."

Didi had forgotten when she made her stage centerpieces that there would also be floral centerpieces. She was a little worried about how it would all fit on the table, but she decided that was one bridge she'd have to cross when she came to it.

"Speaking of tables, I found a wedding rental company that'll give us a great discount on tables and chairs," said Amelia. "They do tablecloths, dishes, silverware—all that stuff."

"How'd you get a discount?" asked Didi.

"I gave them a free ad in my next news video," said Amelia. "Which I'm filming as soon as the wedding's over."

"Nice work," said Resa.

"I just really hope we can get the permit for the gazebo," said Amelia. "Any luck with that, Harriet?"

Harriet had polished off the carrot cake and was gesturing at the vanilla fondant one. "The good news is that my guy can get us a permit, no problem."

"That's great!" Didi's face lit up. She was starting to think the wedding might not be doomed after all.

"The bad news is, someone already reserved the gazebo for Saturday night."

Didi's face darkened again. "That's a no-go, then."

"Can you change the time of the wedding?" asked Harriet. "It's totally open before noon."

Didi shook her head. "Weddings take hours. She can't get married at nine in the morning! And even if she could, most of the wedding party are in her theater troupe, and they have a performance Saturday at ten in the Senior Center."

Harriet frowned. "Well, then you're out of luck, because the person who has the gazebo Saturday night is definitely not going to cancel."

Resa wrinkled her eyebrows. "Who's using the gazebo Saturday night?"

"Val." Harriet plunged her fork into the rich chocolate cake. "She's having a fundraiser for her campaign there."

"You've got to be kidding me," said Resa. She sliced into the chocolate cake with what seemed like excessive force.

"The election's not even for another two months," Didi protested.

Harriet shrugged, her mouth too full to talk.

"I'm texting her right now," said Resa, pulling her phone out of her pocket. "I'll tell her if she doesn't shut this ridiculous thing down—"

Amelia grabbed the phone from Resa's hand.

"No way," Amelia said. "That'll only make her more dead set on doing it."

Didi adjusted her glasses. "I'll talk to her. Tomorrow, at school."

"Didi," said Resa in a "Let's face facts" tone of voice. "That'll never work. You're way too nice."

Didi bristled. It was typical of Resa to assume that being nice was a liability in business. Sometimes being nice was just what was necessary to get stuff done. "You catch more flies with honey" was one of her mother's favorite expressions.

"I'll handle it," said Didi confidently. "You all have helped so much already. I don't know how to thank you."

"Ummm, more cake works for me." Harriet handed her plate over to Resa to taste another cake option.

"Yeah, we're happy to help," said Resa. "It's fun."

Didi shook her head. "I want to split my fee with you."

"Didi!" Amelia protested. "That's yours. You're earning it."

Didi wiped her mouth with a napkin. "We're all earning it. Plus, there's plenty to go around—and you three need the cash, too."

"If you want to give us a little of the money, I won't say no. It would be amazing if I could donate to Bounce Back!" said Resa. "But we're not splitting it evenly—that's just not fair. You take half, and the three of us will split the other half." She extended her hand out to Didi. "That's my final offer. Take it or leave it."

Didi laughed, then extended her hand to shake Resa's. "I'll take it."

"Good," said Resa. "Now finish that cake slice. We haven't reached maximum sugar rush yet."

The next morning, Didi arrived at school so early Val wasn't even there. Ms. Davis registered surprise at seeing Didi, with a Tupperware of cookies in hand, before she'd even gotten the door unlocked.

"Those for me?" she joked, nodding at the Tupperware.

Didi smiled. "Not this time."

At that moment, Val raced in—and nearly fainted when she saw Didi chatting with Ms. Davis.

"Didi," she panted. "You're early."

"Yeah," said Didi. "I wanted—well, actually I wanted to talk to you."

"I'll be making photocopies," said Ms. Davis as she walked out of the room, holding a stack of papers.

Val walked over to her seat in the very front of the room and tossed her backpack onto the table. "What's up?"

Didi, following behind, handed her the container of cookies.

"Snickerdoodles," she said. "Those are your favorite, right?"

Val raised one eyebrow suspiciously.

"I smell butter," she said.

"Well, the recipe calls for a lot of it," agreed Didi.

"No, I mean, I can tell you're buttering me up," said Val, sitting in her chair. "I just don't know why."

"Touché." Didi slid into the seat next to Val. "I have a massive problem, and you're the only one who can help."

Didi knew that Val was the kind of person who liked to feel indispensable, and she thought that by appealing to her expertise, it might make her inclined to help.

Her strategy seemed to work. Val peeled off the lid to the Tupperware and took a tentative nibble. "What's the problem?"

"Well, I know you're supposed to have a campaign party at the new gazebo on Saturday night—"

"Oh, is that it?" asked Val, looking relieved. "Of course you can come. I was just about to send out a massive text invite. You're definitely on the list."

"Thanks, but . . . ," Didi said. This was going to be more awkward than she'd anticipated, but there was no backing out now. "I wasn't going to ask to be invited. I was going to ask you to cancel it."

Val paused midbite, then resumed chewing, only much more slowly. Didi could tell she was not happy with the direction this conversation was taking.

"Why would I cancel a party that I've been planning for weeks?" asked Val.

In a rush, Didi explained the chain reaction that led to her suddenly planning a wedding that was close to being in shambles. "I honestly can't think of anywhere else she can get married," pleaded Didi. "In just two days."

Val chewed slowly, pondering. "That *is* a massive problem."

"I know." Didi stuck her thumbnail in her mouth and chewed at it as she waited for Val's decision.

"I'd offer to brainstorm with you—" started Val.

"Oh, that's okay, you don't have to—" Didi did not think she had the energy for one of Val's intense brainstorming sessions.

"But no need for brainstorming. I already have an idea," Val concluded.

"You do?"

"I haven't sent the invite out yet," said Val slowly. "So I could potentially reschedule my party to next weekend."

Didi felt a surge of optimism flood her. "Oh, Val, that would be so incredibly—"

"Not so fast," said Val, holding her hand up. "You didn't hear my conditions yet."

"There are conditions?"

Val shrugged. "You know what Sheila Orbacher says, 'There's always a price tag, even when it's invisible.'"

"Not you, too?" Didi moaned. Everywhere she turned, Sheila Orbacher was giving her advice.

"Huh?" asked Val.

"Nothing," replied Didi. "What are the conditions?"

"Just one," said Val. "You agree to be my campaign manager."

Didi's stomach clenched up. "Me? Why me? I've never been a campaign manager."

"You can learn on the job," said Val. "What really matters is the ability to stay calm under pressure. And I've seen you do that plenty of times."

"Hey there!" said Resa brightly, breezing in. "Oooh—are those snickerdoodles?" She reached in and grabbed a cookie. "What are you two chatting about?"

"Oh, you know," said Val, "just some early-morning wheeling and dealing."

Didi knew it was just her imagination, but it was almost as if she could feel the pinch of being stuck between a rock and a hard place.

When Didi walked through her front door after school, all she wanted to do was crawl into her bed, pull the fluffy down comforter up under her chin, and sleep.

She couldn't, of course. She could barely find the time to sleep at night, much less in the middle of the day. The list of things to do was endless.

The most difficult item on that list was avoiding telling Resa about the deal she'd made with Val to get her to cancel the party Saturday.

She knew she should feel relieved that Val had

agreed to cancel the party, because now Agnes had a place to get married—and not just any place, but the perfect spot. The gazebo had just been finished, was still in pristine condition—painted a gleaming, hopeful white. The lawn around it was so fresh and plush. It would make a lovely site for a wedding—picture-perfect.

Still, Didi did not feel relieved. It was like she'd traded one heavy weight for another. She had fixed Agnes's problem but had created another one for herself. It wasn't that Didi minded so much being Val's campaign manager. She would have preferred to choose it of her own accord and not be forced into it, but she knew that she'd be a great campaign manager and that Val would make a good class president. But Didi knew Resa would see it as a betrayal.

She tossed her backpack onto the wooden floor by the coat closet, slipped off her shoes neatly, and walked into the kitchen for a snack before she got to work chipping away at her to-do list. If her mother was home when she got back from school, Didi could always count on a tasty snack waiting for her.

"Hello, *beta*," her mother sang. She had poured some crispy bhujia into a bowl and was slicing an apple into perfect wedges to place on a plate. "You look hungry."

Didi washed her hands at the sink, then sat down across from her mom, who smiled at her broadly.

"Agnes called me today," her mom said.

Didi snapped her head up. "Is everything okay? Don't tell me she got sick!"

Her mother laughed. "No, no, she only called to thank me. She said you are doing the most marvelous job. She cannot believe you are only twelve years old. She said you are so much better at the job than that bad-tempered woman."

"Well, that's not saying very much," said Didi, crunching into an apple slice.

"I am so proud of you," said her mother, pushing a strand of hair away from Didi's face. "I am not surprised, of course. You are wonderful at everything you do, my genius girl."

"Thanks, Maa." The more praise her mom lavished on her, the sadder she felt. It suddenly became hard for her to swallow the clump of chewed-up apple in her mouth. She was not wonderful at everything she did, and she wished her mom would acknowledge that. It'd make her feel better when she messed up. Like she was doing right now.

"What is the matter?" her mother asked, her dark eyes filling with concern behind her glasses.

"Nothing." Didi shook her head. "I'm just tired, that's all."

"Indira," her mother said. "You misunderstand

me. Agnes is very happy with your work. You have done a wonderful job."

Didi sighed, feeling like she was on the verge of tears.

"I know, Maa. That's really nice. It's just—"

"Yes?"

Didi looked up at her mother, always so devoted, attentive to each and every one of Didi's needs. Didi had told her she wanted a job, and—presto!—her mother had found her not one but two jobs, had made her more money than she ever dreamed of. She couldn't very well turn around and explain that even though she'd gotten exactly what she wanted, she was discovering it wasn't what she wanted at all. The whole reason she'd gotten involved with the wedding in the first place was to do art, which was something she loved, but now she wasn't doing anything artistic whatsoever. Instead, she was making a million stressful decisions about stuff she didn't care anything about at all, like flowers and napkin colors.

It was just so much responsibility, and the stakes were so high. If she messed up or let something fall through the cracks, this incredibly special day, this day that Agnes and Rick would remember for the rest of their lives, would be ruined.

But the only way out of this was through. And it wouldn't help to worry her mother.

So Didi inhaled deeply.

"Thanks, Maa," she said, biting into an apple slice. She gulped down the apple, then plastered on a wide smile. "That's really nice to hear. I'm glad. The wedding is going to be great."

Didi would make sure of it.

18

Didi woke the next morning to her phone having a meltdown. At least, that's what it sounded like. It was buzzing and dinging and beeping. Then it started ringing.

She blinked open her eyes blearily. She'd been up late working on the seating chart, which was near impossible to figure out. Agnes had given her a long list of people who should be seated together and another long list of people who should be kept apart, and there was no way to make it all fit. Then she had to iron out all the information about the decorations. There were so many little details that hadn't occurred to her—she needed to use decorations that wouldn't blow away, and she couldn't overlook the bridal tent. Plus, how would she light up the seating area after the sun set? She'd gotten to bed really, really late, and now she needed another hour or two of sleep. Her phone, though, would not stand for that.

She raised up on her elbows to look at the screen and felt herself wake all the way up, instantly. It was Resa calling, for starters. And she'd overslept. Homeroom started in five minutes.

Didi jumped out of bed and then froze. She didn't know what to do first—get dressed? Pack up her schoolbag? Answer Resa's call?

There was no way she could get to school before first period started, not even if she sprinted there in her pj's. She'd never been late for school before. Sick, yes, but never late. The prospect of it made her short-circuit.

The door to her bedroom burst open, and there was her mother, in her fuchsia bathrobe, with bed head.

"My alarm!" her mother exclaimed. "It did not go off!"

Mother and daughter stood there for a moment, paralyzed, and then Mrs. Singh yelled, "Get dressed! You will eat on the way!" and raced down the stairs.

In less than five minutes, Didi was grabbing a

banana and piece of dry toast from her mother as she ran out the door. It turned out that if you didn't brush your teeth, comb your hair, or change out of your pajama top, it hardly took any time at all to leave your house.

She was not much of an athlete and couldn't run the whole way to school, but she did speed-walk and managed to race through the door of homeroom just as the first bell rang. She rushed against the current of students coursing out the door and headed to Ms. Davis's desk so she'd be marked present for the day. Ms. Davis gave her a nod and a wave to confirm she'd seen her, and Didi swiveled around to get to English.

And there was Resa. Resa did not look happy.

"Hey," said Didi. "I'm sorry I couldn't pick up the phone this morning. It was a disaster! Would you believe I slept until 8:03? I almost—"

Resa blinked slowly, then tilted her head at Didi in a way that made her look mighty curious.

"Did you check your texts?" she asked.

Didi was flooded with dread. What had happened?

"No," she said. "I didn't even look at my phone."

"Well," said Resa, "congratulations."

And with that, she spun in place and joined the rest of the stragglers exiting the classroom.

Didi knew English was about to start, but she also

knew she wouldn't be able to focus on a word Ms. Rivera was saying if she didn't see what was waiting on her phone. She slipped out of the room, down the hallway, and into the girls' restroom, where she pulled her phone out, locked inside a stall.

The screen was littered with text messages, all of them offering up some version of: "Congrats!"

She skimmed through the the group chat, scrolling to the top, where she saw a group text from Val to what looked like all the sixth grade.

I am THRILLED to announce that I will be running for Class President! Huge kickoff party next Saturday night at the gazebo! Want to volunteer on the campaign? Get in touch with my kick-butt campaign manager Didi Singh!

Didi leaned against the door of the stall, closing her eyes. Leave it to Val to broadcast news she wanted to keep under wraps. She was surprised she didn't hire a skywriter.

The damage was done now, Didi thought. She'd have to get through the morning somehow and explain everything to Resa at lunch. If she recounted how Val left her no choice, surely Resa would understand. Didi wasn't even certain if Resa really wanted to be class president—she'd thought it was just something Resa was doing to get under Val's skin.

But at lunch, Resa sat with Giovanni and Grace at an entirely different table. Resa always sat with

Didi at the same table, by the window, near the door. Always.

Amelia and Harriet were waiting at their usual table for her, but they wore grim expressions. Even when she tried to explain why she'd cut the deal with Val, their hard expressions did not soften.

"You should've at least told her yourself," Amelia said.

"Yeah," agreed Harriet. "So she didn't have to hear it on the group chat."

Didi hadn't had much of an appetite to start with, but now it felt impossible to even choke down a bite. She excused herself and spent the rest of lunch in the art room, working on the wedding seating chart.

On the way up the stairs, she ran into Val.

"Campaign manager!" Val sang. "Did you see the announcement?"

Didi nodded. "I wish you'd told me you were going to blast out a message to everyone."

"I didn't realize it was a secret," said Val, furrowing her brows.

"It wasn't, really . . ."

"Ohhhh," said Val. "Is this about Resa? I know she's running against me—she responded to my announcement. Told me to get ready for a showdown."

"Yeah," muttered Didi. "I just—I didn't have a chance to tell her before she got the message."

Val nodded slowly. "Well, I'm sorry I made problems for you. Really." She seemed earnest. "Look, to apologize, sign me up to help with the wedding this weekend. I took a flower-arranging class at the community college last summer. I'm pretty good."

"Thanks," said Didi. She turned and walked up the stairs to the art room. It wasn't really Val's fault. It wasn't, she guessed, anybody's fault.

It was a lousy day. She couldn't focus on any of her classes, got scolded for daydreaming by Ms. Gallagher in music history, bombed her science quiz, and forgot to hand in her social studies homework, which she'd stayed up late finishing.

Because Resa wouldn't talk to her, Didi argued with Resa in her mind.

I'm sorry, she imagined herself saying. *I really am. But you shouldn't just assume I'm going to help run your campaign. I mean, I have free will, don't I? Besides, what did you want me to do? I had to get the gazebo. Agnes needs a place to get married. I mean, I'm trying my best!*

She was enormously relieved when the last bell rang, ending the day.

There were a million details to take care of for the wedding. She had to contact the wedding party about the rehearsal at the gazebo tonight, and make sure the officiant had the updated wedding vows, then send a message to all the guests, confirming they knew about the change of site tomorrow. She had to swing by Linda's flower shop to look at the daisies and see—

Didi was so lost in thought she didn't notice Harriet approaching until Harriet had hooked her arm through Didi's.

"You're coming with me." Harriet pulled her toward the street corner to the left. It was the exact opposite direction from where Didi needed to go.

"Oh, no, Harriet, I need to get straight home," Didi protested.

"Just a tiny pit stop," Harriet said, pulling her across the street. "For ice cream."

Didi knew resisting Harriet was pointless. Besides, ice cream sounded pretty perfect right now. She was starving.

"Fine," said Didi. "You can help me finish the seating chart while we eat."

But as soon as they walked through the door of the ice-cream shop, Didi saw Resa seated at a table with Amelia. They'd already ordered and were licking their cones. At hearing the door jingle, Resa looked up. When she saw Didi, she stood, like she was going to bolt.

Amelia, though, gently took her arm and guided her back into her seat.

"I'll get you an ice cream," offered Harriet. "Cookies and cream, right? Sugar cone?"

Didi nodded and slid into a cool metal chair next to Amelia. She couldn't bring herself to meet Resa's eyes. Instead, she glanced over at the counter where Harriet was ordering from a grumpy-looking Eleanor.

Eleanor was wearing a short-sleeved, white-collared shirt with an argyle sweater vest. Her wavy brown hair was pulled into two short pigtails, and the bridge of her large, rectangular glasses was covered with a thick piece of silver duct tape.

"So Harriet and I brought you both here so you can work this out," Amelia explained. "The wedding's tomorrow, and we all agreed to work on it, so we need to put this behind us."

Resa snorted. "Fat chance."

"Resa, I'm really sorry," Didi said quickly. "But I didn't have a choice. It was the only way Val would give up the gazebo."

"We could've found another location for the wedding!" Resa exclaimed.

Didi stuck her thumbnail into her mouth and chewed reflexively.

"We really couldn't have," interjected Amelia. "Not in two days."

"Well, then, you should've talked her into something else! A different arrangement!" Resa pulled off her white headband and stretched it absentmindedly. "This is exactly why I wanted to talk to her! You're too nice, Didi! You'll agree to anything!"

Didi felt like she'd been slapped in the face. Her heart raced, and she blinked back tears.

"Resa, you're supposed to be making peace," chastised Amelia.

"You're wrong," said Didi. "I won't agree to anything. Just as an example, I won't agree to working with someone who treats me like you're treating me right now."

Didi's brown eyes flashed behind her glasses. Over the many years they'd been friends, Resa had rarely seen her so angry. She knew that when Didi flared up, it was usually with good cause. It was usually a sign Resa had gone too far.

"One cookies-and-cream scoop!" announced Eleanor, appearing at their table, with Harriet at her side. "Sugar cone."

Eleanor handed Didi the ice cream, then glanced between Didi and Resa. It wasn't a big shop. Arguments that happened there were heard by all.

"I have a thought," she said. "You want to hear it?"

"Sure," said Amelia.

"You can tell a lot about a person from their ice-cream order," she said. "Look at you girls." She gestured around the table.

"Harriet always goes for the new specialty flavors or something big, loud, and colorful." Harriet smiled, having just scooped a large spoonful of Banana Peanut Butter Brittle with mochi and sprinkles into her mouth. "Harriet's a big personality—for better, or worse."

Harriet looked up, briefly insulted, but Eleanor winked at her and added: "Usually better."

Eleanor turned to Resa. "You can try to tamp Harriet down, but if you do, you're taking away her biggest asset—which is her energy and her zest. So let Harriet be Harriet."

"Thank you!" Harriet said, vindicated.

"Whereas Didi here, her ice-cream order never wavers. Always cookies and cream, always a sugar cone. She likes her cones classic, pure, simple, so she can taste the subtle flavors at work."

Didi smiled. "It's true."

"That's how Didi rolls." Eleanor shrugged. "You can force her to be aggressive, but it's just not who she is. And if you do, you're losing her biggest asset, which is her diplomacy."

"Uh-huh," said Resa. She looked skeptical.

"You need to think of your group here as a whole toolbox," said Eleanor. "Full of different tools. You don't want a toolbox full of screwdrivers, now do you?"

"Am I the screwdriver in this scenario?" asked Amelia.

"Totally," said Eleanor. "And you"—she turned to Resa and fixed her with a hard look—"are definitely the hammer."

"It was an accident!" Resa protested. "I *said*, 'Heads-up!'"

"Didi's not a set of pliers, and she's not a saw," said Eleanor. "She's the level. You need a level. Trust me."

The bell on the door jingled as a new customer walked in.

"Hi there," Eleanor greeted them, making her way to the counter. "What can I get for you?"

Resa finished off her cone, popping the last bite into her mouth.

"You're right, Didi," Resa said. "You're not too nice. You're just nice enough. I'm sorry, okay?"

"I'm sorry, too," Didi said. "I should've told you about the deal I made with Val last night, but I . . . I just didn't want to upset you." Didi licked her cone, which always melted more quickly than she, a slow eater, could consume it. "I didn't want to make the deal with Val, but I had to. This whole wedding planning thing—" She sighed. "It's so stressful—I have to get everything perfect because there's no redo option, you know? And, also, I could not be less interested in this stuff—picking dish patterns and arranging table seating. Can a thing be stressful and boring at the same time?"

"Ugh, yes," said Harriet. "Sitting still for portraits."

Didi smiled. "Touché."

"But you're a superplanner," Resa said. "You put together a whole wedding in less than a week. I hope Agnes realizes what a goddess you are."

"Yeah," Didi said. "She's been super happy about what I've done. She's really nice."

"And the money?" Amelia said. "It's a miracle! I'm going to have plenty of cash to blow on clothes and food and stuff when I get to the city to see my dad."

"I guess." Didi bit into her cone and chewed. "I just . . . I don't enjoy doing it, you know? The part I've liked best was making the place cards and centerpieces. I'm really proud of those—they look amazing. But the rest of it—I don't know, it's just been a slog. A lot of work with no reward."

"Hey, I totally get it," Resa said. "It's how I felt about teaching tennis."

"And the feeling was mutual," called out Eleanor from behind the counter.

Resa rolled her eyes.

"Didi, the wedding is tomorrow," said Amelia. "It'll be over before you know it."

"And we'll be with you every step of the way,"

Harriet promised. "Especially the part where the cupcakes get handed out. You will have extra, right?"

Didi laughed. "Thanks, everybody. I just hope it all works out, you know? I just want it to be a perfect day for Agnes."

"It will be," Amelia assured her. But when Didi got up to grab a napkin, Resa, Amelia, and Harriet exchanged concerned looks. With only one day to go, there was still a huge amount of work to do. It was anybody's guess whether they'd be ready.

20

Everything was falling into place.

Didi didn't want to jinx things by saying it out loud to the others, but in her mind, she thought, *I'm going to pull this off. It's all coming together.*

After what felt like eons, Agnes's wedding day had finally arrived. Now, as the first guests started to arrive at the park, Didi stood in front of the gazebo, admiring her handiwork.

She went through her checklist.

Bride?

Agnes looked absolutely captivating in her white lace gown, her dark hair pulled into a complicated updo with little white daisies tucked carefully in. She was stowed away, out of sight, in the bridal tent, along with her four bridesmaids, women from her theater troupe, who wore matching bronze gowns. Didi thanked her lucky stars for Louise, Agnes's older sister and maid of honor, who ran a tight ship. She'd taken care of all the dresses, hair, and makeup, and everything related to the bride's personal needs. The groom, Rick, had shown up with his coterie of groomsmen. Didi had expected them to be in tights and poofy white shirts, but as it turned out, the groom's mother talked him into a tux, and his friends followed suit.

Bride: check.

Tables and chairs?

Didi had met the wedding rental company at nine A.M. and overseen the table assembly and placement of chairs. It was a good thing she'd arranged to meet them so early—as it turned out, they brought only five tables, when she needed seven.

When the first table was assembled, Didi realized with horror that it was much smaller than she'd imagined, and once you set it fully—with ten sets of dishes and silverware and napkins and glasses and pitchers of water and baskets of bread and vases of flowers—well, there wasn't any room left. None. Definitely not enough room for the enormous stage centerpieces she'd spent so many hours constructing.

"Don't you have smaller dishes?" she asked the wedding rental rep.

"You're serving dinner, right?" he asked.

Didi nodded.

"Then you need a standard-size plate. Anything smaller is going to make guests feel like they're giants eating off dollhouse plates," he explained. And then, in case she didn't fully get it, he clarified. "It'll look strange."

So Didi had to make the tough call to nix the stage centerpieces. Instead, she called Hank from Paper Hub, who she happened to know dabbled in calligraphy.

"Got any plans today?" she asked. "I've got an emergency calligraphy situation."

Hank agreed to make up new table-number signs to mount on simple wire holders that could slide right into the floral arrangements. He asked for fifty dollars, and she agreed, thinking she would have paid him a lot more if he'd asked for it. She made a mental note to remember that the next time someone asked her what her fee was. *Start high*, she thought, *and go from there*.

Tables and chairs: check.

Decorations?

Amelia, Resa, and Harriet had arrived that morning at eleven, a whopping five hours before the wedding started, ready to work. Amelia had stopped by the party store and picked up pastel-colored streamers to hang in the bridal tent. Resa had spent most of the night before making paper lanterns to hang over the dance floor. Harriet had gathered together strand after strand of tiny, twinkly white Christmas lights to string up all around the gazebo and the party area. Unfortunately, when Harriet plugged the lights in, half of them didn't work. Harriet was just about to implode when Val waltzed in with the entire student government behind her.

"Just tell us where you need us," Val said. "I've got an army of helpers."

The extra help was sorely needed. Val and the student government leaders tested out strands of Christmas lights to find the defective ones. Then, having discovered Harriet had neglected to bring extension cords, they went on a cord recon mission and came back with enough length of cords to wrap around the entire town. It took hours and hours, not to mention plenty of sweat, but eventually all the lights and streamers and lanterns were hung. The park looked undeniably festive now, and when it got dark, Didi knew, the ambience would be stupendous.

Val even figured out a way to save the stage centerpieces.

"Just put them on the table where you're arranging the place card scrolls," she said. "You can put the scrolls on the stage—and arrange by alphabet.

One stage can hold all the A through F last names, the next will be G through L—you get the idea. It'll be adorable."

It absolutely was. It was even better than the original plan Didi had envisioned.

Decorations: check.

Music?

The Renaissance Skinks had arrived on time, which was probably because Didi, who knew Harriet and her brothers never arrived on time for anything, had set the boys' arrival time for thirty minutes earlier than she actually needed them. They didn't look Elizabethan in the least, but they did look sharp in black suits and blue ties that reminded Didi of their namesake's, the skink's, blue tongue.

Music: check.

Flowers?

Mrs. Singh had saved the day and brought over the most breathtaking bouquets earlier that day. Agnes had gotten the peonies she wanted—three enormous bloodred blossoms, with the white daisies and pink tulips tucked around them. The center-pieces featured the same daisies and tulips, with mari-golds added. They were simple but breathtaking, and Agnes actually ooooh-ed when she caught sight of them.

Flowers: check.

Food?

At the Kings Hotel, Agnes had arranged for Renaissance-style food: banquet tables with massive turkey legs, spiral potatoes, pies. Didi searched the area for a caterer that could replicate this, with just a few days' notice, but she couldn't find one. She apologized profusely when she called Agnes to break the news to her.

"Oh, it's fine," said Agnes. "Actually, I did a little research, and I discovered the food we were serving isn't authentic Renaissance food anyway. They ate stuff like deer and rabbits and pigeons, even herons." She laughed. "And I am not serving herons at my wedding."

Agnes was totally flexible about the menu; she just wanted to make sure Didi had some gluten-free options for Rick's cousin Edwina. So Didi had arranged for a bunch of gluten-free options . . . and vegetarian ones . . . and she had triple-checked there were no tree nuts used in any of the recipes, too. Nailing down the menu was a headache, but now she stood watching the catering company get the platters of hors d'oeuvres ready, and they looked so good Didi's mouth actually started to water.

Food: check.

So with the bride, decorations, music, flowers, and food all settled, and with a large clipboard full of charts and schedules and contact info in her hand, Didi was feeling grand. Amelia, Resa, and Harriet had all headed home about an hour and a half ago to change into their wedding finery, and they would arrive any minute, along with Val, who'd volunteered her help.

Didi stood in front of the gazebo. To her left was the field where the guests would be seated for the ceremony. Five rows of white folding chairs were lined neatly—ten chairs in each row, with a white cloth aisle down the middle. The bride and groom, officiant, and wedding party would stand in the gazebo for the ceremony.

To her right, on the other side of the gazebo, was the field where the party would be held. Six tables had been placed in a circle, with a large empty space in the middle for dancing. The Renaissance Skinks were set up on the far side of the field.

Didi walked down the aisle in the ceremony space. She spotted a chair that was a little too close to the one in front of it and walked over quickly to adjust it before people started to sit down.

"You look beautiful, *beta*."

Didi thought surely the stress of the planning was getting to her and she was hearing things—until she looked up and saw her mother's voice was attached to her mother, who was wearing her favorite evening dress—a silk burgundy gown with black beads around the collar. Her father stood next to her, looking dashing in his best suit.

"Maa," she said, baffled. "What are you doing here?"

"I was invited." Her mother smiled. "You know, your aunt and uncle and the triplets are coming, of course. And Agnes called me last night to tell me what a wonderful job you were doing, and she said it would bring her great pleasure if your father and I came." She raised her eyebrows at her daughter. "I did not want to deny her great pleasure."

"But—" Didi sputtered. "Agnes didn't say anything. You're not on the list."

"Well," said her father, "it is lucky that we know the person in charge of the list."

He winked at her. "Sheila Orbacher was right. She says, 'It pays to know people in high places. Just bring your ladder.'"

She couldn't turn her parents away, of course, but she didn't have enough room for them at the tables—and she wasn't sure she'd have enough food, either. There were exactly fifty chairs, fifty place settings, fifty meals ordered from the catering company Resa's mom had recommended. Didi would have to call the company and see if they could accommodate two more, and she'd have to somehow rustle up forks, knives, glasses—

"Teresa!" her mother called as Resa walked down the aisle to meet them.

"Nice dress," Didi said.

"Look familiar?" Resa shot back.

Resa had borrowed one of Didi's dresses, not so much because she liked it but because she didn't have a single dress in her own closet. Every year, her *abuela* gave her one for Christmas, and every year, Resa handed it over to Didi, who was a big fan of frocks. Didi had enjoyed looking through her closet for one Resa could borrow, and this one—a pale blue boatneck dress with a skirt that flared and a black patent leather belt—was beautiful on her.

"You look lovely," Mrs. Singh told Resa. "Is your mother here?"

"I hope not!" Didi cried out before she could stop herself. The thought of having to finagle two more chairs and meals made her panic.

Resa laughed. "Relax, Di." She turned to Mrs. Singh. "I'm flying solo. My mom came by earlier to drop off the cupcakes."

"We must let the girls work," Mr. Singh said to his wife, and Didi watched with relief as they walked over to two chairs in the front row to sit.

"Can you believe Agnes invited them?" Didi hissed at Resa.

"Uhh, yeah, I can," said Resa. "Since your mom's the one who spoke to Agnes about getting you this job in the first place."

Didi walked away from the ceremony area and pulled her phone out of her purse. She flipped through the carefully organized pages on her clipboard to find the number for the caterer and quickly typed a text message, asking if she could get two more meals added.

Within seconds, the caterer had written back that they always send a few extra meals, just in case. It was fine.

Didi sighed in relief. "Well, that's taken care of," she said, striding to the other side of the gazebo, to where the dinner tables had been set up. "Now let's hope there are enough extra plates and chairs."

Resa followed after her. "I think it's sweet your parents came," she said. "Your mom really cares about you so much."

Didi felt the stab of guilt she often did when she complained about her mom. She was about to reply when she stopped short in front of the first dinner table.

"Look at that!" She pointed to the table-number sign in the middle of the floral arrangement.

"Is it not supposed to say, 'Table 1'?" asked Resa, confused.

"No, it is," said Didi. "Just not so small! I mean, look at how tiny that "1" is! Who could even read that?"

She reached over to grab it, though for what purpose she didn't know. There was no way she could fix it.

"Didi," said Resa, gently putting a hand on her shoulder. "It's fine. Really."

Didi inhaled deeply, then breathed out fast. "You're right. I've got to keep my eyes on the prize."

"You go check on Agnes," said Resa. "I'll look in the box of stuff the wedding rental people left. I bet they left a few extra place settings, just in case."

Didi nodded and turned in the direction of the bridal tent.

She collided with Val, and her clipboard and pen went flying through the air and onto the grass.

"Whoa," said Val, retrieving Didi's things. "Where are you rushing to?"

"Checking on Agnes," said Didi. "Walk with me."

Val was in a short-sleeved silver sequin tunic with black leggings, and her hair was pushed back into a sleek pompadour.

"You look stressed," said Val. "Where do you need me?"

Didi flipped through her clipboard until she found the seating chart. She pulled that page off and handed it to Val.

"This is the seating chart. I am trusting you with it." Didi was staring at Val with a gaze so intense it even made Val, the queen of intense stares, nervous.

"O-okay," she replied.

"Can you figure out how to squeeze two more people into one of these full tables?" Didi asked. "Do *not* touch the bridal table—and whatever you do, don't put Agnes's cousin Marv at the same table as Freddy. There was a big family fight years ago, something about a baseball card. They can't be anywhere near each other!"

"Sure," said Val, looking at the chart. "I'll come up with a few different ideas for you."

Val and Didi froze at the sound of a shout behind them.

"No! I don't need any help from *you*!"

Didi swiveled toward the yelling to identify its source. Nine-year-old Alfie Kim, hands on his hips, was staring down Resa with fierce defiance. In another context, it would have been funny— that tiny boy looking so furious and Resa, a foot taller than him, cowering—but since the argument looked like it was going to flare up into a major scene, Didi was not amused. Resa's tennis coaching just kept on producing more drama—and now was not the time for a showdown.

"I got this," Val assured Didi. "He's my next-door neighbor, so we're pals."

"Are you sure?" Didi didn't look convinced.

"Absolutely," Val said, already jogging over to the

arguing pair. She yelled over her shoulder: "You check on Agnes. It's almost go-time."

Didi watched as Val approached Alfie.

"I can find a seat on my own!" Alfie was shouting. "I'm not in nursery school, you know!"

"Okay, okay," Resa was saying, her hands up in surrender. "Sorry."

"Hey, Alf," said Val. "Great to see you! Are you friends with Agnes? Or Rick?"

Alfie turned to her, momentarily surprised. "Uh, Rick. My mom and his mom work together in the real estate agency."

"So cool!" Val said as Resa slinked away discreetly. "Come here, I've got to show you the cupcake pyramid! It's going to blow your mind!"

Grateful that Val had put the fire out, Didi speed-walked to the bridal tent. Resa appeared beside her.

"Would you believe Val, of all people, just saved me?" asked Resa.

Didi smiled. "Not so bad having her around, is it?"

"Okay, okay, you told me so." Resa rolled her eyes. "Hey, I found a bunch of extra place settings in the box, so we're good. We can just drag over some chairs from the ceremony space to use."

"Good thinking," said Didi. "Val will tell you where to put the plates and chairs. She's got the seating chart."

"You surrendered your seating chart to Val?" Resa raised her eyebrows.

"Are you jealous?" joked Didi, arriving at the entrance to the bridal tent.

"Nah. She's the right person for the job." Resa smiled. "Oh, hey—Amelia texted me. She's running a little late. Had to stop by Harriet's house to help with a 'wardrobe malfunction.'"

"I hope no one was injured." Didi laughed.

"Seriously." Resa glanced down at her phone to check the time. "Ten minutes until the ceremony. Are you good?"

Didi nodded. *Fake it 'til you make it*, she thought.

21

In most weddings, the bride is a nervous wreck and the wedding planner, who's done it a thousand times, is cool as a cucumber. At the Stein/Chan wedding, the roles were reversed.

Agnes, a longtime performer, was in her element, standing before a huge group of people, soaking in the spotlight. Rick, an actor in his own right, was just as comfortable and composed. Didi, however, was all nerves. Before the wedding began, she'd chewed up both her thumbnails and her pointer fingernails and now she was working on her ring finger. If the wedding didn't end soon, she thought, she'd run out of nails.

The officiant was Barry, the director of Bard Without Barriers, a distinguished-looking man with a gray beard that reached to his midchest. He had a sonorous, hypnotic voice and soliloquized beautifully about love, marriage, and friendship. When the bride and groom recited their vows, which they'd written themselves in iambic pentameter, there was not a dry eye in the place. Didi was petrified they'd forget their vows and wanted them to carry a copy with them, but Amelia had assured her that if the couple could commit whole pages of Shakespeare to memory, a few rhyming couplets posed no problem.

Once they'd been pronounced husband and wife, the Renaissance Skinks played a rousing version of "Here Comes the Bride!" with Larry wailing on his electric guitar. Everyone applauded and threw rose petals as they walked down the aisle. Didi's mom had thought of that detail—and since they'd used roses that were damaged or on the verge of wilting, they'd gotten them for next to nothing.

Didi couldn't take a moment to enjoy the relief she felt, though, because she had to find the photographer to oversee the bridal-party photos in front of the gazebo while the rest of the guests enjoyed cocktail hour. She patrolled the perimeter of the ceremony area, scanning the crowd to find him and his oversize camera.

"Didi! It was so—so—" Didi turned to find Harriet standing next to her, blowing her nose into a tissue. "Beauuuuuuutiful!" At this, Harriet began to cry again. Amelia, who stood next to her, put her arm around Harriet.

"The whole time," she mouthed to Didi over Harriet's head.

"True love," sniffed Harriet. "It just—it pulls on your heartstrings." She wiped her eyes with the back of her hand. "You know?"

Didi smiled.

"Sorry we were late," Amelia said. "We made it just after the ceremony started. Found seats in the back."

"I heard about the outfit emergency," said Didi. She scanned Harriet for signs of malfunction, but Harriet looked surprisingly, well, ordinary. She looked more ordinary than usual, in fact, in a pretty white blouse, turquoise pleated skirt, and cute star leggings.

"I am so sorry about my appearance," said Harriet, gesturing at her adorable outfit. "Trust me, it was not my intention to show up tonight looking like this."

"You look great!" said Didi.

"I had this whole amazing outfit all ready," Harriet explained, pushing her braids behind her shoulders. "Cam-Thu helped me with it!"

Cam-Thu was Harriet's favorite, and most stylish, cousin. Fashion was her obsession. She had so many items of clothing there wasn't room in her closet to hold them all. She'd wear an outfit a few times, then give it to Harriet, who was overjoyed to add it to her collection.

"Cam-Thu had this *incredible* gown she wore to the Renaissance Fair a few years ago," said Harriet, her eyes lighting up. "It was purple brocade with gold stitching, and it had puffy white sleeves and this corset bodice that tied up the back, and tons of tulle underneath to make it puff up."

Sounds like way too much, was what Didi was thinking. But instead, she said, "Sounds cool. What happened to it?"

"Zappa—that stinker—got into the garment bag, and he went to town on the tulle!" Harriet's face collapsed, and it looked like she was going to cry again, this time tears of sadness. "He can't be trusted with fluffy stuff like chair padding and tulle!"

"We did it, Di!" Rick, the groom, had walked over and was giving her a high five. She gladly obliged.

"You were incredible!" Didi gushed.

"Thanks." Rick smiled. "Hey, listen, Agnes

found the photographer, and she says it's picture time."

Just then, Resa rushed over with the news that Rick's cousin Edwina was upset because there were no gluten-free options.

"But there are gluten-free options!" Didi moaned. She wished for the umpteenth time since she'd taken the job that she could clone herself so she could manage to be in two places, doing two things, at the same time. Then she realized she had something better than clones, she had the Startup Squad.

"Amelia, I need you to go supervise the photos," she said, pulling a page out of her clipboard. "Here's the list of groups we need to photograph— this list has been triple-checked, so make sure you stick to it."

"On it," said Amelia.

"Harriet, can you go with her and make sure the flower girl and ring bearer are looking at that camera?" Didi knew Harriet had a knack with kids and could hold their attention, which was not a skill many people possessed.

"Your wish is my command," said Harriet, spinning on her heels and chasing after Amelia and Rick.

Didi turned to Resa. "I'll make sure the caterer sends out the gluten-free hors d'oeuvres," she said. "Can you go tell Edwina it's a mix-up and those are coming?"

There seemed to be a million tiny hiccups, missteps, and mix-ups, but Didi sorted each one out without too much difficulty. This was possible because of the fleet of assistants she had, ready and willing to help in whatever way she needed. It was only after all the guests had found their seats, and the waiters began serving dinner, that she could sit for a moment on a chair near the place card display table, drink a glass of lemonade, and take stock of things. She was in the homestretch now, she realized with intense relief. All that remained were toasts, dancing, and cupcakes. Easy peasy.

"Bang-up job, Didi."

A familiar voice cut through her reverie. Didi looked up to find Eleanor in a kelly green dress with a black patent leather belt, her hair pinned back into a low bun that was threatening to unravel. She flopped into the chair next to Didi and sipped her glass of soda.

"What are you doing here?" Didi asked. "You're not on the list!"

"It's great to see you, too," Eleanor replied with a hefty dose of sarcasm. "Don't worry; I'm with the band. They needed help transporting the equipment. I do not need a place setting."

"In that case, it *is* great to see you." Didi smiled. "Hey, you look different. Is it . . . oh, wow, you got new glasses, didn't you?"

Eleanor smiled and nodded. "You like?"

"I love." Didi meant it. The new glasses were oval instead of rectangular, and two-toned dark blue up top, fading into a playful turquoise.

"Turns out, I needed a stronger prescription," Eleanor said. "So it's probably a good thing my other ones broke. I might not have gone to the eye doctor for a while otherwise. And now I can see crystal clear." She opened her eyes wide, as if to prove it.

"So what you're basically saying is I'm a lifesaver." Resa had walked over and now sat down next to Didi. "I'm a godsend. A miracle worker."

"Totally," replied Eleanor, laughing. But her laugh was drowned out by the sound of a blood-curdling scream coming from the middle of the dinner tables.

Didi was on her feet in a flash, racing in the direction of the scream. It was coming from Table 4, from Edwina, who stood on a chair, her hands splayed in front of her like she was ready to fend off an attacker. The rest of the table's guests had abandoned their seats, which made it very easy for Didi to spot, instantly, the source of the pandemonium.

Zappa.

Harriet's best-loved skink (she had quite a few) was standing on Table 4. Right in the middle of a Caesar salad. She was delightedly chomping on a crouton.

Didi was paralyzed by shock.

Harriet, however, was not. She pushed through the little crowd that had gathered to see what the commotion was about.

"*Zappa!*" she bellowed, lunging for her.

At that, the skink, who had seemed peaceful and contented, startled. Her whole scaly body tensed up for a single instant, and then she moved.

The skink was lightning fast.

Didi was sure she'd never seen an animal move faster, not even a horse or a cheetah. Zappa darted off the plate of salad, to the end of the table, then leaped onto the chair waiting there, before skittering down the chair body to the ground.

That's when things got out of hand.

The wedding guests scattered in every direction, crashing into one another, knocking over chairs, and screaming relentlessly.

The loudest screamer, by far, was Harriet.

"*My baby!*" she screeched. "*She'll be stampeded!*"

A high-pitched whistle pierced through the din. Didi looked up to see Resa standing on a chair, her fingers in her mouth.

"*Freeze!*" she yelled as soon as she had everyone's attention.

And everyone did.

"*Everybody stay still!*" Val shouted. She was holding

a flashlight and waving it around under the tables, where it was too dark to see.

That was the thing about Resa, and Val, too. You could say what you would about them, but they were natural leaders. Decisive. Cool under pressure. The kind of people, both of them, who made good class presidents.

With everyone standing still, it took only a second to spot Zappa, who was racing full speed toward the gazebo.

Harriet opened her mouth to scream again, but Didi shhh-ed her loudly.

"She's already spooked," Didi said. "You'll scare her more."

Instead of yelling, Harriet speed-tiptoed, which was not an easy feat, to the gazebo, Didi at her side. Harriet walked up the three steps to enter the gazebo, and Didi walked around to the opposite side.

"Here, skinky skinky skinky," called Harriet softly, reaching her hand out, palm side up.

Zappa, still obviously off-kilter, froze and stared at Harriet for a long second. Then she did a full 180 revolution and raced across the gazebo, directly toward Didi. For a moment, Didi thought the gazebo structure would stop her, but Zappa was small enough to slink right through the wooden slats without even slowing down.

"Oh, no," Didi whimpered. "Not again."

It took every last ounce of courage she possessed to stop herself from sprinting away from the gazebo and out of the park as fast as her tired legs would carry her.

As Zappa launched herself off the floor of the gazebo, headed onto the grass right at Didi's feet, Didi knew what she had to do. She threw herself forward, her arms outstretched, and grabbed for the animal, howling as she did so.

The next thing she knew, she was holding something very squirmy and very cold. These sensations filled her with horror. The only way she ever wanted to encounter a reptile was in a zoo, behind thick, protective glass. And here she was *holding* one.

Didi still recalled with terrible clarity the feeling of having Zappa tangled in her hair, completely stuck and out of reach. To not repeat that awful experience, she pressed the animal to her chest. What happened then was unexpected.

Zappa suddenly stopped squirming. She lay still and suddenly calm on Didi's chest, just like a baby might. By the time Harriet made it around the gazebo to Didi, the situation was under control.

Harriet reached over and carefully relocated Zappa to her own shoulder.

"Didi," Harriet whispered, so as not to startle the skink, "you held Zappa!"

"I . . . did." Didi couldn't quite believe it herself. "I really did."

"I think she likes you!" Harriet observed. As they both watched, the skink stuck out her blue tongue in Didi's direction, just as if she were blowing her a kiss.

For the rest of the evening, guests speculated as to the series of circumstances that led to a blue-tongued skink running amok at the wedding. Some thought she was supposed to be a wedding gift from Agnes to Rick or Rick to Agnes. Others thought the skink had escaped from the zoo across town and had been attracted to the party by the alluring smell of cupcakes. It was Amelia, though, who witnessed what really happened.

"My lips were really chapped, so I went over to the bridal tent where Harriet and I stashed our bags when we first came in," Amelia explained to the rest of the girls later. "And while I was rooting through my purse, I happened to glance over at Harriet's backpack because, out of the corner of my eye, I saw it move."

"Oh my . . ." Harriet's voice trailed off. She understood what had happened.

"And as I watched, a little green head poked out of the corner of the backpack," said Amelia. "I was just reaching out to zip the bag closed and go get Harriet, but my movement scared her, and that's when she burst out of the backpack and out of the tent . . . and the rest is history."

"It's because I put that darn chew toy in my backpack!" Harriet exclaimed. "I was going to see if Alfie could give it to his cousin Francesca, whose father's best friend is my chew-toy client, Gus."

"Sounds like a super-complicated delivery system for a skink toy," said Amelia.

"It does, now that I think about it," agreed Harriet.

Didi heard a tinkling sound of glass being hit by silverware. She looked up and saw Agnes on her feet at the bridal table, a glass of champagne in her hand.

Didi glanced down at her phone to check the time.

"Oh, no! It's not toast time yet!" Didi moaned. "We still have another ten minutes!"

"I know it's not officially toast time yet," Agnes was saying, as if she had heard Didi's words. She'd gotten to know Didi well in the last week or so. "But I had a little extra toast I wanted to make."

Agnes turned toward Didi and the girls. "Today was made possible by an incredible wedding planner—the most organized, patient, determined, and resourceful person I've ever met—and to think, she's only twelve!"

The crowd laughed, and Agnes winked at Didi.

"Indira Singh, you saved the wedding!" Agnes announced. "Thank you so much!"

The crowd erupted into applause. Didi turned scarlet, embarrassed by the attention, but loving it, too. She hadn't been expecting this.

"And thank you to her backup, too—Amelia, Teresa, and Harriet!" Rick was adding. "Or, as they're known nowadays, the Startup Squad!"

There was even more applause. Harriet, never one to shy away from an ovation, jumped to her feet and took a bow.

Resa yelled back: "Don't forget Val!"

"And Val, of course!" Agnes shouted.

When the applause died down, Agnes added: "In addition to making this wedding amazing and, um, *unforgettable*—"

The guests tittered at this.

"They have also made us go viral!" Agnes grinned. "If you go on ImageFest, you will see we're the number one trending video right now."

Didi looked at her friends. "No!"

Amelia had already opened the ImageFest app on her phone and was staring, eyes wide, at the screen. "Yes!" She handed Didi the phone, and the girls crowded around to see.

There, on the screen, was footage of Zappa leaping off Table 4, darting into the gazebo.

"It's me! It's me!" Harriet squealed when she spotted herself saying, "Here, skinky skinky skinky."

"Oh, Didi, look!" Resa said, as the on-screen Didi, squeezing her eyes tight, lunged for—and caught—Zappa.

Every guest who had a phone within arm's reach had pulled it out and was watching the video. Whoops and hollers and claps erupted, and then the wail of Larry's guitar sound and the Renaissance Skinks, sounding decidedly rock and roll, played "For She's a Jolly Good Fellow" in honor of the ladies.

"I can't believe Agnes isn't mad," Didi said to the girls when the fanfare subsided. "I thought for sure I'd ruined her wedding."

"She's an actress," said Harriet, as if she were stating the obvious. "She wants fame—and you just got it for her."

"Mom alert," said Resa. "Ten o'clock."

Didi looked up to see her mother heading straight toward her.

"Indira!" Her mother, beaming, grabbed her hands. "I have the most wonderful news! I was sitting at a table with a very nice young woman—Lorraine, I think, or Lori or Lucinda." Her mother shook her head, as if the woman's name was of no importance. "This young woman just became engaged—"

Resa could see where the conversation was headed. Without knowing it, Mrs. Singh was racing toward a head-on collision with Didi. Resa tried to steer the conversation in another direction.

"How cool!" Resa interjected. "Hey, what did you think of those vows? Pretty amazing, huh?"

"Uh, yes," said Mrs. Singh hurriedly. "But the thing I wanted to tell you is, this young woman would like to hire you as her planner! And I negotiated for you, so your fee will be even higher this time!"

Didi flushed with sudden, intense frustration.

"No!" she snapped. "I'm not doing it!"

Resa, who had been anticipating the explosion, turned to the other girls. "Hey, can you help me with the cupcakes?"

Within a few seconds, the girls made themselves scarce, leaving Didi alone with her mother.

"Indira," Mrs. Singh chastised. "What a way to speak to your mother."

"I know," Didi said, looking down at her hands.

She hated snapping at her mother, and that she had done it in front of her friends made her feel even worse. "I'm sorry."

"I don't understand why you are upset," said Mrs. Singh, taking the seat next to Didi that Resa had vacated. "Everything has gone very well. Now you will have an even better job, with even more money."

"Look, Maa, I'm glad everything went well, but that doesn't change the fact that I didn't enjoy any of this," Didi said. "I was so stressed out the whole time."

"Because it was your first time," Mrs. Singh persisted. "Next time will be easier."

"Yeah, sure, maybe," said Didi. "But it's not really that it was hard, Maa. When I made that monochromatic acrylic painting for art last year, that was really hard, and sometimes I got stressed out, but I liked doing it anyway. When it was over, I felt satisfied. I wanted to do it again. This is different. All I feel is relief. It's just not for me."

"Maybe you should sleep on it," Mrs. Singh suggested. "Tomorrow, when you have rested, you may change your mind. Agnes says you are the best in the business."

Didi inhaled deeply, then breathed out through her nose. Her mother was right. If she was being honest, she knew that without her determination, problem-solving, and organization skills, the wedding would have been canceled. She was good at planning.

"That's probably true," she said. "But maybe, you know, maybe that's not the most important part. I mean, I may be good at planning, but if I don't enjoy it, shouldn't I spend my time doing something else? Something that I love? Like making art?"

Mrs. Singh didn't say anything for a few long moments. She took off her glasses, wiped them clean on her scarf, then placed them carefully back on her face.

Mrs. Singh smiled tenderly at her daughter. "Yes, *beta*. Yes, of course."

"You're not . . ." Didi looked down at her patent leather shoes. "Are you disappointed?"

"Indira, I could never be disappointed in you." Her mother pulled Didi into an embrace and hugged her for a long time. Didi melted into the hug. She felt terrifically relaxed for the first time in a long time.

"Next time," Mrs. Singh said, pulling back. "You tell me sooner."

"The thing is," Didi said, "I didn't know I didn't like it until I tried. So I'm glad you got me the job. I'm glad I tried it." She laughed. "I just don't think I'll be doing it again anytime soon."

"I will tell Lorraine," said her mother. "Or Lori or Lucinda."

Didi smiled as her mother stood and headed back toward her table. After taking a few steps, though, Mrs. Singh turned back to Didi.

"Oh, *beta*, I must thank you," said her mother.

"For what?" Didi asked.

"I have never gone viral before," Mrs. Singh said with a smile.

"Eeeeeeeeew!" Harriet moaned, her mouth full with a brussels sprout slider.

"It's not that bad," said Didi, chewing slowly.

"Ugh," groaned Resa, looking down at the brussels sprout slider on her plate. "Just the smell! I can't even take a bite."

"I love them," said Amelia, reaching for another.

"Are you joking?" Harriet had spat hers into a napkin and was filling her glass full of lemonade so she could rid her mouth of the taste.

"Nope," said Amelia. "I love brussels sprouts."

"Then you take them home," said Didi.

"I mean, I will, but that's an awful lot of sliders for just me and my mom." Amelia looked at the huge platter of sliders in the middle of Didi's table. There had to be at least twenty on the plate, all left over from the wedding the night before.

"I only ordered these to have a few gluten-free options for Edwina," said Didi. "And she didn't even eat them."

"Can you blame her?" asked Resa, laughing.

"Are there any cupcakes left?" asked Harriet. "Because I would definitely take those home with me."

"Nope," said Didi. She had her laptop open on the table in front of her and was typing. "Sorry, Harriet."

"Whatcha doing there, Di?" asked Amelia. "Watching our Skinks Gone Wild video again?"

"No," said Didi, looking at the screen. "I think forty times was enough. I could reenact the whole scene from memory." She clicked the Finish button on the screen in front of her.

"Done!" announced Didi. "I am now the proud owner of PictureHouse."

The other girls whooped and cheered.

"Can you do my portrait on that?" asked Harriet excitedly. "I bet it'll take way less time."

"Absolutely," said Didi. "I'll do a portrait of all of you. And maybe one of all of us together—we can use it as a profile pic for our website."

"Ooooooh, a website is a great idea," said Resa.

"Yeah, and I can design it with this software, too," said Didi. "I want to use cool tones, you know—some deep indigos, maybe periwinkle, possible some slate gray."

"Ahhhhh, there's the Didi I know and love," said Resa. "Geeking out about colors."

Amelia laughed. "Yeah, you seem way more relaxed since the wedding ended, Didi."

Didi grinned. "I really am," she said. "I'm glad we did it, because, well, it turned out great—"

"And we're internet-famous now!" pointed out Harriet.

"And we're flush with cash again," said Resa. "I made a hefty donation to Bounce Back! this morning."

"Yeah, I texted my friends in the city and told them to go ahead and get those concert tickets," Amelia said. "I'm so excited!"

Didi's phone buzzed in her pocket. She pulled it out, read the text she'd just received, and laughed out loud.

"It's Gigi," she said. "Asking if I'm looking for an internship this summer. She'd consider taking me on, for a small fee."

"She must be feeling better if she's texting," said Resa.

"Hey, you all want to come to the new dog run

with me?" asked Amelia. "The one they just opened on Pecan Street?"

"Yes!" Harriet exclaimed. "You had me at 'dog'!"

"Are you thinking about getting a dog?" asked Resa.

"No," said Amelia. "I'm thinking about doing a news video on it, though. And since we're all internet-famous now, I thought you three might want to help."

"Can't," said Resa, standing up. She tossed her slider into the trash. "I'm going to meet Val."

"Val?" asked Harriet. "Redheaded, Olympic-level gymnast Val?"

"That's the one." Resa put her coral-colored sweater on and buttoned the front. "There is the small possibility that we may be . . . I guess you could call it 'collaborating.'"

"On what?" asked Didi. For the life of her, she could not possibly imagine what Resa and Val could collaborate on without clobbering each other within five minutes.

"Class president," Resa said. "Val said she might consider me for VP, and I told her fat chance, but if she played her cards right, I might let her be my VP." Resa shrugged. "We'll see what she has to say. A meeting couldn't hurt."

"If you teamed up, I could be *both* your campaign managers," said Didi.

"I know," said Resa, eyebrows raised. "I'll see what I can do."

"Meet us at the dog run after?" asked Amelia. "You can bring Val if you want."

"Sure," said Resa. "I can do some research while I'm there."

"Research?" asked Harriet. "On what?"

Didi saw Resa's eyes twinkle with the spark of a new idea.

"Oh, I've just got something simmering," she said with a smile. "And when it's ready, the Startup Squad will be the first to know."

Welcome to

THE STARTUP SQUAD®

You can start your own business by yourself or form a Startup Squad with your friends! The best businesses are based on something that you are interested in. So first, think of what you love to do and how you can turn it into a business that you'll love to run. Then, do market research to make sure people will be willing to pay for your product or service. Finally, think through everything about your business and create a business plan. Here are some tips from the Startup Squad that will help make your business a huge success!

Turn Your Passion into a Business

Think about what you're interested in—like art. Or animals. Or the environment. Or fashion. Start a business that involves something you already love, and you'll have more fun and be more motivated to turn it into a *big* business. Didi made a lot of money and was successful in planning Agnes's wedding, but she wasn't passionate about it. She realized she'd much rather start a business that focused on art.

Next, think of a problem you can help solve that's related to your interests. For example, if you like animals, you'd love to spend time with dogs. A problem some dog owners have is that there's no one to take care of their dogs when they're away from home. So you could start a dog-walking business!

If you love to bake, you'd like a business where you can make lots of breads and sweets. People love freshly baked cookies, but not everyone has the time or talent to bake cookies themselves. So you can start a baking business!

You can also start a business related to a cause that you're passionate about, like helping the environment. So you can start a business making environmentally friendly soaps or organizing volunteers to pick up litter around parks and nature preserves.

Your business doesn't have to be a new invention. Some entrepreneurs start businesses because they want to improve a product that already exists—like making a more enjoyable video game, a healthier pet treat, or a more environmentally friendly backpack. Look around and think, *What can be improved?*

👍 Market Research

Market research is gathering information about who might be interested in what you're selling, and what competition is already out there. Market research is also how you check to see if there are enough people interested in your product or service that you can earn a profit. Harriet matched her passion (skinks) with a market problem (there weren't any skink chew toys), which was great! But she didn't do any research to find out how many people owned skinks and would be interested in actually buying her product. Turns out: not enough to make it a profitable business.

You can learn a lot by doing market research. For instance, how many people might want to buy your product, what kind of customers you should look for (what age group, what other interests they might have), which similar products or services already exist, and how much you can charge for what you're selling. The internet is a great place to start doing market research. Search for companies and products similar to yours, check the cost of supplies, learn about potential customers, determine the size of the market, and much more.

You can also create a survey of questions about your product or service and get direct feedback from people. Start by asking your family and friends. Then, with an adult's help, reach out to other potential customers whom you aren't related to. But make sure to ask everyone to be honest with you! It won't be helpful at all if they pretend to like your product because they don't want to hurt your feelings. If they give you honest feedback, you can change things for the better before you even start.

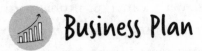 Business Plan

A **business plan** describes in detail how you want your business to operate, its goals, and its plan to achieve those goals. It's a road map to guide you as you start your company. Creating a business plan allows you to think through all aspects of your business so you can avoid mistakes before you make them. Amelia created a business plan to figure out her business, and it helped her appear professional when she pitched her idea to local businesses and the local newspaper's staff.

You can find a business plan template online at thestartupsquad.com/stuffyouneed that will help you plan your business. It includes sections such as:

★ Motivation: What's Your Why?

★ The Big Idea: What Problem Will You Solve?

★ Target Audience: Who Are Your Customers?

★ "It" Factor: What Makes You or Your Product Different?

★ Name Your Business: Make It Memorable

★ Create a Slogan: Make It Catchy to Catch Customers!

★ Competition: Who Else Is Doing Your Thing?

★ Money Matters: How Will You Make a Profit?

★ Customer Research: How Will You Make Sure People Will Buy Your Product?

★ Advertising: How Will You Talk About What You're Selling?

★ Sales Pitch: What Will You Say to People to Convince Them to Buy Your Product or Service?

Want our favorite recipe for lemonade and more tips about running a business? You can find all that and more in the first two books in The Startup Squad series. And you can learn more about running your own business at thestartupsquad.com. Start planning your empire, because GIRLS MEAN BUSINESS!

About the Authors

Brian Weisfeld has been building businesses his entire life. In elementary school, he bought ninety-five pounds of gummy bears and hired his friends to sell them. As a teen, he made and sold mixtapes (ask your parents what those are), sorted baseball cards (he got paid in cards), babysat four days a week after school, and sold nuts and dried fruit (and more gummy bears) in a neighborhood store. As an adult, Brian helped build a number of well-known billion-dollar companies, including IMAX Corporation and Coupons.com. Brian is the founder and Chief Squad Officer of The Startup Squad, an initiative that empowers girls to realize their potential and follow their dreams, whatever their passions. Brian lives in Silicon Valley and can often be found eating gummy bears with his wife while watching his two daughters sell lemonade from the end of their driveway.

Nicole C. Kear grew up in New York City, where she still lives with her husband as well as her three kids, who are budding lemonade moguls. She's written lots of essays and a memoir, *Now I See You,* for grown-ups and *Foreverland* and the Fix-It Friends series for kids. She has a bunch of fancy, boring diplomas and one red clown nose from circus school. Seriously.

Meet a real-life girl entrepreneur!

Simone Bridges is the founder and CEO of Goddess Food Factory (goddessfoodfactory.com), a fun-filled bakery and STEM/STREAM company.

Q: Tell us about your business.

A: Goddess Food Factory teaches kids science, technology, reading, engineering, arts, and mathematics using culinary methods. Our company sells traditional baked desserts, apparel, bedding, backpacks, educational baking kits for kids, and more. I also founded a nonprofit (simonebridgesinspires.org) that promotes STREAM education and youth entrepreneurship.

Q: How old were you when you started, and where did your idea come from?

A: My grandmother, Phyllis, taught me how to bake

when I was only three years old. At nine, I started selling treats to our church family, neighbors, and several friends. I opened Goddess Food Factory when I was eleven.

Q: What's the most fun part of running a business?

A: I get to meet new people every day. I listen to their success stories and challenges. Another favorite thing is having a place for kids to come learn about STEM/STREAM.

Q: What's the hardest?

A: One difficult aspect is not being able to register for certain baking classes due to age requirements.

Q: What are your future plans for your business?

A: My future goals include hosting more events for underserved youth and empowering them to discover their inner superpowers. I'm writing my first cookbook, and I want to empower kids to *bake the world a better place*!

Q: What tasks take up the most time to run your business?

A: Flying across the country for speaking engagements and to conduct food demonstrations. I spend a lot of time writing and practicing speeches and traveling, but I enjoy it all.

Q: Do you have a role model or mentor?

A: Besides my grandmother and my mom, Chef Kenna is my mentor and a huge inspiration.

Q: What was the biggest mistake you made? What did you learn from it?

A: 2018's Ms. Corporate America, Elizabeth Garcia, owner of Elizabeth's Secret Beauty Bar, asked me at a business event, "Why aren't you wearing one of your shirts with your brand on it?" Since then, I stay branded.

Q: What do you like to do when you're not conquering the business world?

A: I'm dancing to my favorite songs, hanging out with my friends and family, and eating my favorite foods while binge-watching great movies.

Q: Any advice for other girls starting a business?

A: My message is simple: Start today. I saw my grandmother making money from her baked items, so I started making cookies and charging a quarter. I didn't realize at the time that I already had a small business.

Want to learn about other girl entrepreneurs?
Go to thestartupsquad.com!